EINSTEIN MEADOWS ¿QUÉ PASÓ?

Lessons Learned While

Letting It All Hang Out

By Ned and Nancy Engel

EINSTEIN MEADOWS ¿QUÉ PASÓ?
Lessons Learned While Letting It All Hang Out

By Ned and Nancy Engel

ISBN: 978-0-9966233-3-9 Print book
ISBN: 978-0-9966233-4-6 Kindle eBook

The authors may be contacted at Einstein Meadows Press
createmiracles@einsteinmeadows.com

Photo credits:
Front and back cover desert landscape by Gene Hanson,
www.genehanson.com

Front cover Woodstock bus by: Jaime Martorano,
www.jaimemartorano.com (faces added by the authors)

Front and back cover original design by: the authors

Front and back cover digital production design enhancement by: The Highland Studio, Cold Spring, NY www.thehighlandstudio.com

Printed in the U.S.A.

Inspirational Thoughts from Our Favorite Childhood Authors

"Who says nothing is impossible? Some people do it every day!" – Alfred E. Neuman

"Life is too short to be living someone else's dream."
– Hugh Hefner

"The secret of getting ahead is getting started."
– Mark Twain

"All we see or seem is but a dream within a dream."
– Edgar Allen Poe

"Anything one man can imagine; other men can make real." – Jules Verne

"The world is full of obvious things which nobody by any chance ever observes." – Sir Arthur Conan Doyle

"Logic will get you from A to B. Imagination will take you everywhere." – Albert Einstein

ACKNOWLEDGEMENTS

This sequel would not have been possible without the support of family, friends, acquaintances, and all our marvelous readers. It's been great to write a second novel together! We have met many people who marveled about how a marriage could survive such a quest. Our secret is that after 40 years together, we are still best friends and cosmic twins. Ned believes I can do anything – including write a novel – which I thought was impossible. He empowers me to reach for the stars and beyond.

We owe a special thank you to Ms. Roxy Lohuis-Tejeda, the Senior Programs Supervisor at Key Biscayne Community Center in Florida, who gave us a chance to present our first novel.

We were also fortunate to have met Judi Koslin, who hosts jewelry making classes at the Center. Judi knows everyone, and introduced us as "Ned and Nancy, the authors". Judi's friend Liz Portuondo taught us some Spanish and made some thoughtful suggestions for the next novel. These contacts led to an invitation by Pamela Parker, the activities director of the Palace in Coral Gables. As we bicycled or walked all over Key Biscayne, where we were vacationing, people asked about our progress on the sequel. They were curious to know what our neighbors out west were up to, and how the story would unfold.

We were ready to leisurely start writing when we arrived back at the Meadows. Margaret, a Goodreads reviewer, wondered whether we had an application to screen people who wanted to move into the neighborhood. Coincidentally when we returned home, the developer Scott Gonzaga asked us to help create just such a questionnaire. Irwin Kalman, my friend since junior high school, came up with some gems; although they might not pass muster with the Fair Housing Act. Nevertheless, the Meadowites loved his suggestions. You will find them in Chapter 3.

We should also thank my brother Stephen for coming up with a creative investment idea (sex robots) for the community. It has sure been a crowd pleaser and a money maker. You can make money too – just read Chapter 2. We were encouraged to keep writing after my sister Lenore gave copies of our novel to her fellow psychiatrists. Now that took guts!

We give a shout-out (all the way to Canada!) to Hannah Verrassing who really enjoyed our first novel and eagerly anticipated the next installment of life at the Meadows. Our friend, Dr. Dave Giannascoli appreciated the sequel's focus on epiphanies and encouraged us to highlight the Einstonians' personal growth. Thanks also go to Dawn Zichko and Dirk Geithner who suggested possible cover illustrations; and shared ideas about environmentally sensitive architectural improvements, which our neighbors appreciated.

Our friend, Barbara Morris's interesting anecdotes about dealing with disruptive denizens have been very useful in keeping the peace among the Einstonians. We also thank everyone at Einstein Meadows, without whom there would be no story to tell.

And, finally, my deepest gratitude to my grandmother, a natural psychologist, whose faith in me led to many years of scholarship and service to others.

CHAPTER 1–

Welcome Back To Einstein Meadows

Welcome to the sequel of Einstein Meadows: The Unspoken Perils & Thrills of Living in a retirement Community. If you read the first novel, you are probably wondering what's happening now. Are the Meadowites (Einstonians) still smoking, getting naked and feeling frisky? Of course! In this novel, you will discover that medicinal marijuana leads to enlightenment for the denizens of this wild, wacky, and unpredictable neighborhood.

Now, let's bring you up to speed. Last time we ended with a cliffhanger. Sister Misty Pashkudnik, our resident blogger and staunch opposer of the weed, had attempted to burn down the entire grow. Luckily, her roommate, Brother Gunther called the sheriff who arrested Misty. However, while Sheriff Mortimer and Deputy Maurice were enjoying donuts and coffee, Sister Misty escaped from the squad car. (Of course, Dr. Freud predicted that Misty would break loose. In fact, he told Ned that it was a pity the police did not bag her. He added rather crudely, "You have more to worry about from her than you do from the Feds interfering with the grow.")

Naturally, the Einstonians are very concerned about their crop in case Sister Misty shows up with matches. They installed a state-of-the-art CCTV system to cover the main access points to the Meadows. And, the Einstonians hired armed guards. No one knows Sister Misty's whereabouts. But we all know she may return to finish the job. Do you smell something sweet burning?

So, who lives in the Meadows? We will start with Dr. Freud. Not to be confused with the internationally famous father of psychoanalysis. Our Dr. Freud stepped out from a parallel universe after Ned challenged one of the community's Nobel Laureate physicists to create a vortex. How's that for the power of intention? In our novel, Dr. Freud has hung up his diploma as well as most, but not all, of his undergarments. He replaced his cigar with an authentic peace pipe. Black socks and a bow tie are still de rigueur. Dr. Freud always likes to have the last word. (There are some who think this is a cultural trait.)

Dr. Freud: "Wait a second; wait a second. Dr. E., you didn't give me a chance to share my thoughts on Sister Misty's clinical diagnosis."

Ned: "How is that important now? She escaped, remember?"

6

Dr. Freud: "What makes you think she won't be back? I believe she has melancholia with occasional mania, is sexually repressed, and a generally obnoxious woman. She even refers to her cute dog as evil. You two have some *chutzpah* by writing a sequel to Einstein Meadows without giving me the last word in your first novel. Where is your respect for elders? You should be ashamed. What would your parents say?"

Nancy & Ned: (in unison) "It's our novel and we decide who gets to speak!"

OK enough of the foreshadowing! It occurs to us that you our paying customer may not have read our first novel, or may have already forgotten it. (Of course, that would be very hard to believe, unless you are seniors like us.) Therefore, you may not be aware of how the residents of Einstein Meadows liberated themselves or even who they are.

Here is a brief synopsis of the novel that inspired this genuine sequel. (But you should still buy the original.) *Einstein Meadows: The Unspoken Perils & Thrills of Living in a Retirement Community* (www.einsteinmeadows.com) relates the incredible adventures of a group of clueless seniors, and how we shepherded them to the promised land. After much kicking and screaming, the retired academics eventually saw the wisdom of becoming growers and sellers of medicinal marijuana. We affectionately called them ganjapreneurs or Einstonians.

The weed transformed most, but not all, of the residents by freeing them from financial and emotional constraints. Aside from making piles of money, the Einstein Meadowites evolved into better functioning, more fulfilled people. They rode around town in a Woodstock bus, hosted transgender weddings, got naked and generally had a good time. Now, we know that some of you may think we stretched the truth a bit. As strange as it may seem, our story is mostly true, somewhat true, or at least partially true. We let our readers decide.

Of course, it wasn't nonstop partying. The Einstonians also created the Einstein Meets Esalen Institute, a holistic learning center to broaden their ways of understanding and to provide community service.

Nancy and I donated a bronze plaque to mark the entrance to the Institute. We had it inscribed with these powerful words: "The person who has lived the most is not the one with the most years, but the one with the richest experiences." We believed that this sentence written by Jean-Jacques Rousseau in the 18th century perfectly foretold the new enlightened state of our neighbors.

Nevertheless, it would not be Einstein Meadows without some ongoing power struggles and bickering. Surely, you did not expect the road to Shamballa to be as soft as rice paper. It was more like stepping on hot coals and then trying to walk through a room filled with molasses. Do we still have officious board members? Of course. Who doesn't? Marijuana is not a treatment for Trump Derangement Syndrome (TDS), but it might make it a little easier if one of those poorly informed voters lives next door. You can just light up and pretend they disappeared, got bit by a rattlesnake or a rabid coyote, eaten by a wild boar, or kicked in the butt by a jackass. Or, buy them copies of our novels or give them magic brownies as a peace offering; just don't expect a thank you.

As some of you may know, consuming weed often spurs creativity, makes it easier to write satire, and helps folks see life in a new perspective. The Einstonians were no exception. Since we were all advancing in age, it occurred to us that we should start to keep records of our epiphanies lest we lose them to our slowly fading memories. What epiphanies you ask. In the last three years, our formerly staid academentians gained epic amounts of collective wisdom. Thus, in the spirit of bettering the world, in this novel we will reveal some of our neighbors' more high-minded nuggets. Just because we were all getting older doesn't mean we have to resign ourselves to the harsh realities of life or hide in a basement bunker like some presential candidate.

We know the Einstonians are better than that, especially since they are already living an enhanced life. The journey is always easier when you do not have too much baggage. And, we are naked! Plus, the sacred plant is keeping everyone's memories intact and our reasoning as sharp as a rusty nail.

Oops, I almost forgot to tell you about each of the characters in this sequel. Nancy wisely pointed out that not everyone who reads this book will have read the original novel. That would be like reading the New Testament without having read the original version (Old Testament). We hope you enjoy this sequel enough to buy our first book. So, let's review our returning cast of characters. We once met an author of detective novels who reminded us to always keep our strong characters because they add to the continuity. Plus, they're our neighbors anyway.

Well, we are certainly not opposed to beating a dead horse to death; especially since most of the Einstonians have evolved into better functioning people thanks to the magic of cannabis and their own efforts, of course. But this time we add a new twist. Since no one is perfect, you can expect some backsliding (two steps forward and three back). Despite some relapses, they pick themselves up and keep up their forward momentum. This is after all a psychological novel disguised as a satire.

We suggest you return to this introduction periodically so that you can visualize our characters as real people. This task will become much easier when these novels are turned into a television series or movies. A Broadway play would be nice too! So here is a brief reminder of our return players in order of their appearance:

Nancy: My beautiful princess bride is the happy driver of the Woodstock bus, and she is also on the back cover. Who would believe we have been together for more than 40 years? She still looks like a teenager. And of course, she is a great writer and editor.

Brunnhilde Meeskeit: She is a rather tall, masculine looking woman who likes to take charge by officiating at homeowner's meetings. She was the perfect choice to play Dr. Frank-N-Furter for the dinner theatre production of "Rocky Horror Picture Show" in our first novel. Brunni has mellowed out a little since she became an ordained minister who savors the wonder of marijuana.

Zachariah Denker: Zach is the thinking man's man. I always enjoy my conversations with him. A true intellectual – reasoned, patient, scholarly, courteous. At

6.5 feet tall, he towers over most people – except for Brunnhilde.

Ned: Resourceful, creative, and fun. Just look at the man on front cover standing next to the burning bush wearing a Moses costume. Now that's a transformation, considering he was a gun-toting sheriff on the cover of our first novel. He had thought about wearing his six guns. But that would be an anachronism, not to mention totally inappropriate. Who needs guns when you have seen the light? (Only kidding.)

Filbert der Dorftrottel: Every neighborhood has someone like him. He is a self-proclaimed environmental specialist who has something to say about every project on community property. Picture a bald man with an earring in one ear. He has a very loud voice and a great deal of difficulty expressing himself – not unlike some politicians. Is it because of a language-based learning disability, too much drinking, falling out of trees, or being dropped on his head as a baby? Your choice! Wait until you see who he marries.

Ben Chardonnay: Do you have a neighbor who likes his booze? Ben now enhances his wine with high THC marijuana oil. He is a retired academic who loves giving lectures on cruises, especially since his wife doesn't join him due to sea sickness. When he is back at the

Meadows, Ben laments about having to sleep in a different bedroom. But his pet lama, Randy-Candy, seems to appreciate him.

Lillian Lemishkeh: It must have been a rip being one of her graduate students. She just loves talking to her horse. Lillian has perfect posture and is very fit. With her waist-length hair flowing all around her, she looked like Lady Godiva when she rode in the Einstein Meadows equestrian events. Soon you will learn about her sailing and dumpster diving adventures.

Dr. Coconut: One of the two neighborhood medical directors for the community's health center. He reminds me of Dr. Zorba from Ben Casey. He is short with wiry hair.

Buford Swindler: His last name says it all. It's strange to have a financial officer who doesn't know how to add. We'll just chalk it up to aging. Buford was originally a staunch opponent of the "evil weed". Who says you can't teach an old dog new tricks?

Leopold Spieber: He loved to stand up whenever I spoke at HOA meetings and always found a way to contradict whatever I said. Not exactly the most broadminded of neighbors. You probably know someone just like him.

Bella Blozkop: Single and vivacious. Formerly a famous dark-haired rocker, she appeared at Woodstock in 1969. She loved to tell everybody she was a retired physics teacher; I was the only one who knew her secret. Bella is hyperactive and ultra-talkative. My neighbors fondly call her Telstar.

Jeannette Gedankenlos, Psy.D.: The other psychologist in the neighborhood. It took her three times to pass the licensing exam. I prayed for anyone who was her client. It would be sinful and just plain wrong to address her as doctor.

Siegfried Zynismus: Siegfried is a charming fellow, an outspoken HOA board member, and the community cynic. He was less than thrilled when I proposed growing medical marijuana since he didn't vote to approve it in our state.

Chief El Guappo: My *lantsman*! His tribe manages the casino at the Meadows. A proud Apache with a weathered and rugged face.

Ava Sinnlich: Another vivacious babe in the neighborhood. Who says senior can't be lookers? Ava is our resident artist who skillfully helped the Einstonians transform a plain yellow school bus into our own Woodstock bus.

Ima Khazzer: Some say the Lord isn't kind when he gives out looks. Poor Ima looked just like her pet pig. And she enjoyed eating! A true power player at the Meadows. Anyone who disagreed with Ima lived in fear that she would either lift you high into the air or sit on you. She was also rumored to have a wicked punch.

Ms. Lilith: She moved into the neighborhood when a sheriff's eviction was taking place. If you've read the Old Testament, you will know what Ms. Lilith might be up to. We are afraid to describe what she looks like because we don't want to turn to stone.

Professor Growmore: He helped get the original community garden started by volunteering his college co-eds and buff boys to work in the garden. That made him a very popular fellow with the *alter kockers.*

Scott Gonzaga: Our adle-brained developer who was overly impressed with the ivory-tower academentians.

Dr. Ray Rising Sun: Retired Native American lawyer. The ultimate aging hippie with waist long gray hair – sometimes knotted in a pony tail. Women wouldn't hang out with him in the hot tub because he undressed them with his eyes.

Dr. Quackenbush: One of two medical directors at the Meadows. A serious stoner!

Reverend Vernon Verschwender: His favorite saying, "The South will rise again," may prove to be prophetic.

Brother Gunther Shaygetz: Brother Gunther has a reputation for a being a drama queen. Dr. Freud diagnosed him as having a bipolar disorder.

Sheriff Froussard: A scaredy-cat law enforcement officer who prefers eating donuts to doing his job.

Rabbi Kaplan: The brother of Reverend Vernon. How curious and strange that two brothers are clergy representing different faiths.

Jose Maximilian San Carlos de Cortez: Our neighborhood handyman who secretly set up cameras in someone's sex dungeon.

Cara and Karl Chasid: An old married couple who love to bicker with each other.

Sister Misty Pashkudnik: Sheriff Froussard arrested her at the end of our first novel for setting fire to the grow. She escaped from the squad car before she could be involuntarily committed to Briarwood, an insane asylum.

We have added some new characters to spice things up:

El Sabio: He is a very bright, talking chihuahua with distinguished looks. Even though he is a psychiatrist, he prefers to be called by his first name. If you think dogs can't talk, just watch some stoner movies.

Marguerite Ingenieux: The topless sailor who is an expert in dumpster diving. **Judge Solomon** loves to send people to Briarwood, his favorite insane asylum. **Delilah and Scarlett** are well-endowed sex robots. We also introduce a frustrated chambermaid and a hotel manager. We will save their descriptions for when they appear.

Before our first novel was published, we gave the residents of Einstein Meadows a chance to comment. Although we did not know what to expect, everyone was happy to put in their two cents. Of course, some of their reactions were more positive than others. They certainly were honest! When our neighbors learned we were writing a second novel, they volunteered to read the prepublication book and enthusiastically responded. Look for the Residents' Reactions in Chapter 12.

In keeping with our goal of gently educating our readers, we have again included a Yiddish dictionary, which appears after the Residents' Reactions. You'll find italicized words sprinkled through the novel. If you're curious about their meaning, just look them up in our Yiddish dictionary.

And, at the end of the book, we have included the Einstein Meadows 2.0 Pop Quiz. We don't want anyone to strain their brain, so we encourage you to keep the book open. And, if you must, peek at the answer key at the end of the quiz. Top scores will earn you an honorary doctorate in the discipline of your choice. So, read carefully to prepare. Compete with your friends or find a study buddy.

Turn the page and we will share the 10 epiphanies that our stoned and naked seniors discover. Remember, marijuana leads to enlightenment! By spending more time at Einstein Meadows, you will discover how the denizens are no longer wearing out their britches or the soles of their shoes.

Nancy: "That's because they are mostly naked and barefoot."

Dr. Freud: "Yes, but you can still benefit from their insights. There is plenty to learn from your high wattage neighbors."

Mystery voice: "And, what about their collective unconscious?"

CHAPTER 2 –

He Who Makes No Mistakes
Never Makes Anything

We were rolling in the green after we harvested and distributed our initial grow. So, we now have no HOA dues. What an incredible relief that is! Suddenly the Einstein Meadowites faced a delicious quandary – what to do with the hundreds of thousands of dollars of profit reaped from our cash crop after we satisfied the ongoing operating costs of the Meadows. As luck would have it, our neighbors received immediate feedback from the Einstein Meadows Investment Club, whose members were eager to put the surplus green to work.

Even before we became ganjapreneurs, the Investment Club was very popular. However, as soon as the first cash crop came in, we had to find a much larger room for the meetings. So, we moved the monthly meetings from Brunnhilde's living room to the Ponderosa Room. (As you might expect, Brunnhilde still needed control, so she played hostess.) To maximize our financial gains, we pooled our investment capital together.

Brunnhilde Meeskeit: "Thank you all for coming. I see one new face today. Welcome Lilith; we are pleased that you joined us. Welcome back Nancy and Ned; how was your summer? And, today we have a special guest. Chief El Guappo asked to observe our meeting this morning, which I agreed to since he and the Apaches so generously funded our initial grow with the casino. Moreover, they are great business partners.

"We have three items on the agenda to discuss. But, before we get down to business, Nancy graciously brought cannabis cupcakes topped with green icing and sprinkles – which always provide food for thought – and I made coffee to wash them down." (Brunnhilde passes the cupcakes around and takes a bite of one.) "I assume I won't need my gavel today. Zach, would you start the discussion, please?"

Zachariah Denker: "Good morning, neighbors. Since our new neighbor Lilith joins us today and the snowbirds have returned, I thought I would take a few minutes to review the status of our portfolio.

"Obviously, marijuana-related industries represent the bread and butter of our Investment Club. Who knew growing green could be so much fun? Unfortunately, the feds don't allow banks to handle cash from marijuana producers. Brunnhilde, Lillian, and I tapped a few of our neighbors to study several companies which relate to the distribution of medical marijuana. Lillian subscribed to *Cannabis Investing News* as a research tool for the library.

We discovered Leafly, which reviews the best medical cannabis strains and lists dispensaries – all of which represent focused investment opportunities. We are also analyzing a Canadian company called Medical Marijuana, Inc."

After Zachariah updated the group on marijuana related industries, Ned had the floor to discuss the second item on the agenda.

Ned: "Thanks, Zach. I think we're building a good foundation here, but I would like to branch out. I propose a new and different area to research. Last night, Nancy and I were reading the *New York Post* online…"

Filbert der Dorftrottel: (interrupting) "Wait a minute. I thought you only read *The New York Times*."

Ned: "Not since they fired my favorite managing editor several years ago."

Dr. Freud: "*Oy gevalt*! Where are the standards today? No wonder that paper became a radical left rag."

Ned: "We read an article about a company that is developing robotic sex dolls."

Ben Chardonnay: "Now that sounds interesting. Finally, our pinko New York friends came up with an idea we can all jump on."

Nancy: "You're right, Ben. Ned thinks sex dolls will replace dogs as man's best friends. Plus, you don't have to feed, train, or walk them. And, they won't tear up the furniture or ruin your floors."

Filbert: "What's more, they don't smell. I cannot believe I'm saying this, but I think you two are on to something. In fact, maybe everyone will want to buy two dolls. Personally, I would buy three because I like variety. I'd buy a blonde, a brunette and a Vietnames-ish babe with long, black hair to remind me of the great times I had during R & R in Nam."

Lillian Lemishkeh: "I think we should buy several to start a lending library of sex dolls."

Dr. Coconut: "Great idea Lillian. But who is going to be responsible for keeping their privates clean? As you all know, STDs are on the rise in senior communities – especially in Central Florida. We need to maintain proper hygiene here."

Lillian: "Way to go, buzzkill Coconut. However, we live out west! That's a degenerate east coast problem."

Dr. Coconut: "What happened to the good old days when mothers reminded their sons to wear their rubbers?"

Ben: "Ned, what's the name of this company?"

Ned: "The one we read about is called Roxxxy from True Companion. The company's motto is Always Turned On and Ready to Talk and Play."

Ben: "Well, how much do they charge for these bad girls?"

Ned: "Between $7,000 to $15,000, but they expect the prices to drop considerably once the sex dolls are mass produced."

Filbert: "That's a bit steep."

Lillian: "Fine; go buy a sheep, Filbert. Remember, folks. We've got money to burn."

Ned: "Wow, I'm thrilled you are all on top of this investment. The good news is that the TrueCompanion company is offering a special introductory price of $5,000 for each Roxxxy sex doll. If you want to look them up, their website is www.TrueCompanionTV.com."

Ben: "Now, that's more like it. We can afford to buy several to try out before we decide to invest."

Lillian: "I'll pledge $20,000 from the library's budget to get the ball rolling."

Zachariah: (turns to Dr. Quackenbush) "Do you think you could prescribe one for me to help with my erectile dysfunction?"

Dr. Coconut: "If Quackenbush won't, I will. That way we should all be able to write them off on our taxes and get Medicare to foot the bill."

Brunnhilde: (slamming the gavel and dropping her cupcake) "You *alter kockers* are nuts. Medicare will never cover this. They don't even cover prescribed marijuana. You will just have to pay the piper out of pocket."

Buford Swindler: "Come on folks, we're talking about a huge investment opportunity. We have piles of green cash to clean here. Do we really want big government intruding in our affairs and our wallets?"

Nancy: "The article also mentioned an International Congress of Love and Sex with Robots. I suggest we send a delegate to this year's Congress in Amsterdam."

Ned: "And, as luck would have it, the Love and Sex Congress is meeting at the same time as the Cannabis Cup."

Leopold Spieber: (eagerly jumps up) "I volunteer to go to both."

Buford: "As chair of this investment group, I obviously will lead the delegation to Amsterdam."

Brunnhilde: "I wouldn't be surprised if all the pervs in this neighborhood would want to go on this field trip."

Bella Blozkop: "I'm OK with the marijuana investments. However, I'm not sure about these sex robots. I don't think this is a healthy sexual outlet. Nothing beats the real thing."

Lillian: "How come they don't make boy sex dolls? Why should you guys have all the fun?"

Jeannette Gedankenlos: "I think that's a good idea, Lillian. I'll buy at least one male doll."

Filbert: "We prefer girls who don't talk – just moan and groan."

Jeannette: "A mayonnaise jar would be cheaper. Filbert, are you sure you don't want to buy a tranny doll?"

Filbert: "Now there's an idea. That might be great fun – I need a lot to hold onto. Maybe we can ask them to make a custom hermaphrodite just for me. Then I can have the best of both worlds."

Jeannette: "You are a genuine pervert! You need sex therapy. I can find some quality surrogates for all of you degenerates. Who is interested?"

Deafening silence . . .

Filbert: "No, I'm just certifiable."

Dr. Freud: "I don't think he means kosher."

Siegfried Zynismus: "So what have we all decided?"

Zachariah: "I've got the solution. Actuarial data is always superior to clinical judgement. I will make a spreadsheet to compare the performance of the companies we're thinking about."

Dear Reader,
Stay tuned. When the delegation returns from their junket to Amsterdam, we will let you know whether they decided to invest in the sex robots.

Chief El Guappo: "Ms. Meiskeit, is it OK if I address the group? I know I'm just a guest, but I have something important to say."

Brunnhilde: "Sure, but it's Meeskeit, not Meiskeit."

Chief El Guappo: "Listen, my white brothers and sisters. It seems some of you may not be aware of the old Hebrew saying: '*Tafasta meruba lo tafasta.*' It's from the Talmud, so take it seriously."

Leopold: "Talk American, Chief!"

Chief El Guappo: "Fine. Loosely translated, it means 'He who grabs too much grabs nothing at all.' May I remind you millionaires, I am the only billionaire in this group. Put that in your peace pipe and smoke it."

Dear Reader,
You may wonder how an Apache chief speaks
Hebrew. Obviously, if you had read the first novel,
you would know the answer. No worries; this is
easy to solve. Simply go online and buy the
original Einstein Meadows. It's available through
our website: www.einsteinmeadows.com. We
appreciate the business and could use the money.

Peace and love, Ned and Nancy

Ava Sinnlich: (purring) "I think it makes perfect sense to invest in the sex toy industry. I hear the vibrators market is worth more than $2.5 billion a year."

Filbert: (in a challenging voice) "Who told you that?"

Ava: "Just ask Ima. She ought to know."

Ima Khazzer: "Mind your own business, you hussy."

El Sabio: *"What about ben wah balls?"*

Mr. What: "Who said that?"

Everyone looks around for the mystery voice which seems to come out of thin air.

Brunnhilde: "There is one more item on today's agenda. Lilith, you have the floor."

The Monged Mongrel® Line

Ms. Lilith: "Thank you, Brunnhilde. Most of you probably remember that we had to incorporate a service component into our university jobs. Now that we are retired, we can do community service for profit. I propose we allocate $100,000 to the development of The Monged Mongrel® line of pet treats. Why not let our four-legged friends share in the benefits and fun of cannabis? I have already asked Professor Growmore to help us cultivate the strains. With the group's permission, Professor Growmore will give you some background."

Dear Reader,
You remember Professor Growmore. He's the
guy from the local college who brought in buff,
young scantily clad students to help us with the
grow. He retired early on his profits from the
custom blends of medical marijuana he
nurtured; and now lives in Einstein Meadows.

Professor Growmore: "Thank you for the introduction, Lilith. I am so pleased to be speaking to you today as a neighbor and newly retired professor. I have just finished unpacking and I'm settling right into my new home here in the Meadows. After Lilith approached me with the Monged Mongrel idea, I did some research. He hands out business cards.

"The potential for gourmet pet treats is huge. Today, dogs enjoy the elevated status of family members in many households. Folks shell out big bucks for doggy day care, spas, gourmet food, personal pup trainers, designer sunglasses and accessories – even psychotherapy. Some pet owners go so far as to buy a second dog as a companion for the first. Marijuana dog treats are no-brainers. For dogs that are too lethargic "Hair of the Dog" will put the pep back in their step."

Filbert: "Hey, I'll try that too! You know I have a friend who used WD-40 on his knees and it worked, so why wouldn't medicated doggy treats work for me. After all, don't they say dogs are man's best friend?"

Brunnhilde: "Filbert, you need to lay off the sauce."

El Sabio: *"Oh, si, si! We deserve the best. The marketing tag line can be mellow your dog out with these gourmet pet treats. Plus, ours will be kosher because Reverend Verschwender's brother Rabbi Kaplan will inspect and certify the process. Maybe we could get the doggy line into the Israeli marketplace. Do they have* mesheguna *dogs in the Holy Land? Oy! What a mitzvah it would be to sell Monged Mongrel marijuana to Israelis for their doggies."*

Professor Growmore: "What was that? I thought I heard something. I suggest the sales line: Mellow your dog out with these gourmet treats. And I think we should expand into the Israeli market. The mystery voice is right!"

Lilith: "My Wilfred could certainly use some anti-anxiety medication. I volunteer him to be the first test pup. The neighbors have been complaining about his incessant yapping. I tried to tell them that is just the way Pomeranians communicate. Nevertheless, they are not buying it. At least he'll be safe in the lab. I don't want Wilfred to suffer the fate of my former neighbor's dog. We eventually learned that someone took him across the river to a different county, removed his dog tags, and brought him to an animal shelter. That poor dog was never to be seen again.

"And to keep the peace, I'll pledge $100,000 of my own cash to develop the Monged Mongrel® line."

Dr. Coconut: "I think that's a great idea. Just as weed docs recommend different blends and doses of medical marijuana for different human ailments, I'm sure canine maladies require equally varied cannabis concentrations. Am I right Professor?"

Professor Growmore: "Absolutely. I took the initiative and started playing around in the greenhouse after talking to my buddy who is a veterinarian. Balancing the levels of THC and CBD from various strains and working on the dose for edibles, I have come up with seven potential blends of indicas and sativas: Weed Hound, Hair of the Dog, Baked Biscuit, Poochie Pal, Ganja Goodie, Bodacious Bow Wow and Woofer's Delight. Since Lilith has volunteered Wilfred, I will work on Baked Biscuit first. That should mellow him right out."

Filbert: "What about Hair of the Dog?"

Professor Growmore: "Sorry Fil. That will have to wait. I intend to develop this line for animals first. Down the road we'll see if they work on humans."

Brunnhilde: (muttering under her breath): "Give me strength with these diversions and sidetracks. I hope I wasn't that bad when I was drinking." She bangs her gavel. Then speaking aloud to the whole group: "Thank you Lilith and Professor Growmore and everyone else for your research. I move to accept Lilith's proposal to invest $100,000 of her own money in the Monged Mongrel line of medicated pet treats."

Ned: "I second it. If ganja goodies will shut Wilfred up, that's as good as money in the bank for me."

Brunnhilde: "We've heard lots of great ideas this morning. Now it's time to wrap up this meeting. Lillian has pledged $20,000 of library funds for some robotic sex dolls that will be available for folks to borrow. . ."

Dr. Coconut (interrupting): "Still a big ick factor for me with the cleaning of the dolls' woohoos. But, maybe, that's just me."

Brunnhilde: "And our contingent of pervy Ph.D.'s will go to Amsterdam to check out that sex conference."

Bella: (whispering in Nancy's ear) "I'm sure their wives will appreciate the break when the guys are away."

Ned: "Don't forget the green team will also visit Amsterdam for the Cannabis Cup."

Brunnhilde: "I haven't forgotten them, Ned. I believe the Monged Mongrel gourmet pet treats will yield huge cash returns. And, the robotic sex dolls are certainly a game changer. Both sound like great moneymaking ideas."

31

Siegfried Zynismus: "Hold on. You are all moving too fast. Surely, someone remembers when our group portfolio lost $200,000 two years ago. I think we might be getting too far ahead of ourselves to commit cash before we have fully done our research. Just because we have money to burn doesn't mean it all has to go up in smoke."

Filbert: "Yeah, but we hadn't yet started investing in novel industries."

Lilith: "I wasn't here to experience that big loss, mercifully. However, my grandmother always said 'He who makes no mistakes never makes anything.' One thing we can all agree on is that Bubbie knows best. I move that we accept all proposals presented today."

Ima: "Not before I snag another one of those delicious cupcakes."

Brunnhilde: "So moved, I second the motion. Meeting adjourned!"

Dear Reader,

Although it is in the realm of possibility, we haven't heard of any HOA-run community with the facilities we enjoy, and no dues. How about you? Do you know of any functioning (and we use that term loosely) utopian communities with no homeowner's association dues? Please enlighten us and let us know. Send an email to: createmiracles@einsteinmeadows.com

CHAPTER 3 –
What Other People Think of You
Is None of Your Business

Who knew that after Einstein Meadows reached full build-out we would still have such hullabaloos? If you thought the Great Marijuana Debate (which we featured in our first novel) was ridiculous, wait until you read this. Our neighbors created a rigorous screening procedure so posers wouldn't invade the community.

If nothing else, the Einstonians were consistent. Not wanting to be impulsive (as if!!), they weighed all the pros and cons of every issue. That's why Dr. Freud continues to call them the mental masturbators of the universe. Scott Gonzaga, the developer of Einstein Meadows, convened a task force which solicited questions from everyone in the neighborhood. He then scheduled a meeting of the Sustainable Growth and Development (SG&D) Committee to present our neighbors' questions. As you would expect, some of the questions were outrageous not to mention downright illegal.

As people enter the Ponderosa Room, Brunnhilde puts "Long Time Coming" by Crosby, Stills, Nash, and Young on the CD player; and then shares marijuana-infused soda. Jeannette Gedankenlos brought bagels with marijuana butter to spread on them - a new and welcome twist to the traditional New York 'schmear'.

Ben Chardonnay: "Do you have any wine to go with these delicious treats?"

Brunnhilde: "It is only 10 o'clock in the morning and today is Sunday, Ben. You know, we can't serve alcohol until noon."

Scott: "It's been a while since I've attended a meeting. Now, I see why you folks accomplish more these days. Pass me a bagel, please. And would you spread some magic butter on it?

Jeannette Gedankenlos: "As our resident psychologist, I think we should have some common agreement about what types of people we'd like to have and, even more importantly, not have as our neighbors."

Ned: "Excuse me lady, but you aren't the only licensed clinician here."

Jeannette: "Dr. E., I know you are licensed and board certified, but after all, you've been retired for more than a dozen years."

Dr. Freud (whispering in Ned's ear): "She's a real piece of work. It took that loser three times to pass the exam."

Ned: "At least I passed the licensing exam the first time. I think we should ask everyone here what they would like to see."

El Sabio: *"I'd like to see lots of naked bodies."*

Brunnhilde: "Who said that?"

Dr. Freud: "I think there must be a ventriloquist among us."

El Sabio: *"That would be me dummkopf."*

      Suddenly El Sabio becomes visible. El Sabio is a chihuahua with gray hair on his chest. He wears round glasses and has very expressive eyes, which you can't always see under his huge sombrero. Plus, he can make himself invisible when the mood strikes.

Dr. Freud: "Get away from me you little *pisher*. I don't want to catch your fleas."

El Sabio: "Con permisso, Dr. Frudito? We shorthaired beauties from south of the border do not have fleas. On the other hand, you two-legged, hairy beasts are much more likely to carry those nasty pests. I am not the one always scratching my cojones, or sporting a bushy beard."

Dr. Ray Rising Sun: "I'd also like to see naked bodies. I only wish I had better vision."

Nancy: "Listen, Ray; Einstein Meadows is not a nudist colony yet. We're just clothing optional."

Filbert der Dorftrottel: "I want to include a question that determines if the applicants are environmentally friendly."

Dr. Coconut: "The heck with that. We want to make sure they don't have any STDs."

Dr. Quackenbush: "I second that. Unfortunately, not everyone always remembers to wear their galoshes."

Reverend Vernon Verschwender: "And, we need to make sure we don't let in any of those folks with the You-Know-Who Derangement Syndrome that the reliable reporters on the 'Fair and Balanced' network are always talking about."

Brother Gunther Shaygetz: "Holy smokes, no! That's all we need. As if we don't have enough idiots from New York here already!"

Zachariah Denker: "Let's be scientific and just ask the applicants which network they rely on for news."

Ned: "Yeah, I don't think the folks who watch the Comical News Network will fit in here since we all own guns and like to wear them even when we are naked."

Brunnhilde: (waving her gavel, and taking a bite of a bagel) "Enough. You folks take off on more tangents than our so-called representatives from Congress."

Heckler: "I think we need a regime change. It's time for a revolution!"

Reverend Vernon: (under his breath): "I knew we should have seceded."

Heckler: "Can I have an amen? The South will rise again!"

Dr. Freud: "It sounds like you're setting up some sort of quotas; that's too restrictive. I'm sure most of the Einstonians already here would not meet these new standards."

Ben: "You bet it's restrictive. We're rolling in such a pile of bucks from the grow that we must be a little choosy. We all share in the profits, and there should be a limit to our largesse."

Ray: "Dr. Freud is right. Quotas may not fly. We should create an application which follows the Fair Housing Act to the letter."

Reverend Vernon: "We'll do no such thing. This is the Wild West and we are on the verge of seceding anyway. We decide who lives here, not some useless bureaucrats in D.C. We want to be sure we have the right type of people in the Meadows and we don't care what other people think."

Ned: "We particularly don't want those mindless socialist types like the ones who ruined New York City, Portland, Seattle, and southern California. We know where their votes got us last time."

Ray: (starts singing, 'It's the end of the world as we know it') "As the Einstein Meadows senior barrister, I concur with Zachariah. I think you miscreants belong behind bars, or at least in the neighborhood stockade."

Brunnhilde: "What a great idea. We haven't used the stocks in a while. I'll bring some stones."

Nancy: "Let's concentrate on reviewing the proposed questions, then invite the entire community to vote on the application."

Reverend Vernon: "Since when did this neighborhood become a democracy? I thought this was an oligarchy, albeit half-baked at times. Why would we give the rabble any decision-making ability, especially you New Yorkers from our low-rent district?"

Nancy and Ned: (jumping up to sway arm in arm and sing) "These little town blues are melting away. We'll make a brand-new start of it in old New York. If we can make it there, we'll make it anywhere. It's up to you New York New York. Dot dot dota dah. Dot dot dota dah…"

Song fades away. Ned and Nancy continue to sway for a few more beats, hug and smooch, then take their seats.

Ray: "As the only person in this room schooled in justice, I agree with Nancy. Now I know why my ancestors scalped your relatives. You need to get monged more often. I suggest next time we get together, you come in a better state of mind. Here, would you like to take a few puffs from my vape pen?"

Reverend Vernon: "Do you have some of our own custom blends in that pocket-sized peace pipe?"

Ray: "Of course, that's all I ever smoke." (Reverend Vernon takes a few tokes.)

Reverend Vernon: "On second thought, Nancy's right."

Brunnhilde: "OK, let's whittle down this mishmash of neighborhood questions to the top 20."

The community rejected three of Jeannette's favorite questions: Were you breast-fed? If yes, what age were you finally weaned? What age were you toilet trained?

Buford Swindler: "Hold on. What about an application fee?"

Reverend Vernon: "That's easy. $10,000."

Ray: "Whoa, Reverend! That is extreme, but completely reasonable considering what we offer. Be aware, however, that under the Fair Housing Act, we must refund the fee if we nix the applicants."

Buford: "Just make sure we hold on to the application fee long enough to earn interest.

Dear Reader,
The cover letter and questionnaire that the
SG&D Committee finally agreed to send out are
on the next three pages. What do you think
about these questions? Did we cover all the
bases? We would love to hear your reactions.
Don't spare our feelings; just lay them on us –
good, bad, or ugly!
   Email your comments to:
createmiracles@einsteinmeadows.com (Yes,
this is a working email address.)

* EINSTEIN MEADOWS – HOME OF THE ~~ROCKIN'~~ MONGED SENIORS *

Dear Prospective Homeowner,

Thank you for your interest in our special community of Einstein Meadows.

As you know, we have a long waiting list. That is why we require prospective buyers to complete the following questionnaire and submit a $10,000 application fee to assess their suitability to become our new neighbors.

We assume you know that although we are not officially a naturist community, we embody clothing-optional practices. In addition, we are proud to have one of the largest medical marijuana dispensaries in the Southwest, which provides relief to thousands of satisfied customers. Therefore, we impose no restrictions on people using marijuana whenever they choose, anywhere in the Meadows. If either of these unique lifestyles concern you, Einstein Meadows would not be the neighborhood for you.

We recognize that some of the questions may make you feel uncomfortable. You may even believe some of them are too intrusive or illegal. Tough! If we don't think you have what it takes to live among us, that is your loss and our call.

If we like what you write, we will invite you to a personal interview. (*Please note, we will question husbands and wives separately as well as together.) The good news is that you do not have to wear your Sunday best for that occasion. You can even show up naked; just bring a towel to sit on. We appreciate your efforts.

Sincerely,

The Einstein Meadows

Sustainable Growth & Development Committee

* EINSTEIN MEADOWS –
HOME OF THE ~~ROCKIN'~~ MONGED SENIORS *

1) Why did you choose Einstein Meadows?
2) Who referred you to Einstein Meadows?
3) With what political party do you affiliate?
4) What gender do you identify with?
   Circle all that apply. A: Male B: Female
   C: Bisexual   D: Transgender E:
   Pansexual F: Freakazoid
   G: Other
5) What is your highest level of academic achievement?
6) Do you support the full legalization of marijuana?
7) Are you comfortable being naked in public or seeing other people in the buff?
8) Would it make you uneasy to know that some of your neighbors may be swingers?
9) Do you have parties or entertain often?
10) What do you do in your spare time?
11) Where are your ancestors from?
12) What was your last interaction with an attorney?
13) Would you volunteer for one or more committees?
14) Are you interested in serving on the Homeowners Association Board?
15) How much do you weigh?
16) How tall are you?
17) What is your golf handicap?
18) Do you know how to ride a horse?
19) Do you support Second Amendment rights? If so, what is your weapon of choice?
20) What is your net worth?

*Please see the list of supporting materials we require. *

* EINSTEIN MEADOWS –
HOME OF THE ~~ROCKIN'~~ MONGED SENIORS *

Please Include:

    - A bank and brokerage account statement

    - A copy of something you wrote that was published

    - An au naturel photo of yourself. We promise not to post the picture on the Internet.

    - Four personal references

    - A certified bank check for $10,000 made payable to Einstein Meadows Corporation. We will refund the application fee if you are not a good fit for our community. No hard feelings.

Thank you for your interest in Einstein Meadows.

**P.S.: You will experience many epiphanies if you are fortunate enough to live among us. This application represents one of these key lessons: 'What other people think of you is none of your business.' This sentiment will come in very handy if you settle here.

Ned: "If this application is an example of being enlightened, I am truly frightened!"

Jeannette: "With all due respect, that's *bupkes*."

Dr. Freud: "Vaht?? I'm not sure I understand your meaning. Please clarify."

Reverend Vernon: "I think we should try it out. What do we have to lose? Who cares if they are offended?"

Ben: "I'll drink to that. Wait a minute; I'll vape to that. Ray, pass the pocket-sized peace pipe please."

Ned and Nancy: (in unison, laughing) "Try that five times fast. Pass the pocket-sized peace pipe please, pass the pocket-sized peace pipe please, pass the pocket-sized peace pipe please . . .

Nancy: "But, seriously, Ray, send that peace pipe over here."

The Sustainable Growth & Development Committee adjourns.

El Sabio, Dr. Freud, Ned and Nancy hang around for another bagel.

El Sabio: "Uno momento, por favor. I will not be cancelled! I concur with Ned (I mean the Dear Reader author). Soon, you will have more brains and more money than the rest of the retirement squad."

Dr. Freud: "Don't they know the people who gossip reveal more about themselves than the people they are trying to burn?"

El Sabio: "You got that right, Dr. Frudito. It's amazing how many people suffer from insecurity and attempt to unload their troubles on their unsuspecting neighbors."

Ned: "They are just losers. They're the same people who gravitate toward HOA leadership roles. Pay them no mind."

Dr. Freud: "So, to summarize: what other people think of you is none of your business."

Ned: "What he said!"

Piles of applications arrived. The committee unanimously agreed on most of them – either giving them the green light or stopping them short at the gates. The SG&D committee reconvened to discuss the more contentious applications. One potential property owner was very unhappy with the decision on his application. Here's what he wrote:

Dear Einstein Meadows SG&D Committee,

> *I cannot understand why my application to purchase property in your fine neighborhood was rejected. I remember clearly stating that I love to walk around in the nude on my property. Maybe I shouldn't have shared that I wear a propeller beanie.*
> *Could the fact that my photo clearly shows I'm an albino have anything to do with my rejection? Am I too white for y'all? Or is it the fact that I look like a long-haired version of Alfred E Neuman?*
> *How about that I'm an outspoken proponent of gun confiscation? Or lastly, because I'm a skateboarder?*
> *What gives? I hope you snoots will have the decency to respond. I thought I was a perfect fit.*

Clueless in California

Reverend Vernon: "Whoa! Who does this guy think he is? We better respond to this one. We don't want anyone filing a Fair Housing lawsuit. And we certainly can't let him think he's the victim. When it's we who dodged a bullet by sensibly rejecting him. Nancy, would you please draft a response."

Buford: (sighing) "I guess I'll have to return his application fee."

Nancy: "I'll be happy to write this guy."

Brunnhilde: "Try to be kind. We don't want to be soul crushers."

Dear Clueless,

*Clearly your values don't match
ours. We wish you all the best and will
pray for you to come to your senses. If and
when that happens, and that's a big if, take
a long walk off a short pier.*

*For the record, your propeller
beanie wasn't a problem. We were happy
to see that it was MAGA red; and gave you
some bonus points for that. However, all
things considered, it's time for you to
come out of the basement and get a life.*

*Thank you for your interest in
Einstein Meadows.*

*Sincerely,
The Einstein Meadows
Sustainable Growth & Development*

Reverend Vernon: "That's perfect, Nancy. I move to send it out as is."

Brunnhilde: "I second the motion. Buford, cut the check, please. Don't forget to send it at the end of the month so we earn the most interest."

Dear Reader,

     Depending on your political persuasion, you may think that Einstein Meadows is filled with 'deplorables'. Particularly since we enjoy a hedonistic lifestyle. But the reality is that we are an open-minded, clothing-optional haven for 'unconquerables'. Only the brave may join us.

     <u>Remember</u> – What other people think of you is none of your business!

     What could possibly happen next?

CHAPTER 4 -

Be Careful What You Wish For

If you've lived in a retirement community for more than a couple months, you are probably aware of neighbors who have made complaints to the Homeowners Association and gotten frustrated with the way HOAs micromanage grievances. Unfortunately, human nature being what it is, some people get preferred status – especially if one of the persons involved in the complaint is a board member, a confidant, or a big benefactor (donor).

The residents of Einstein Meadows always considered themselves unique compared to people living in other senior neighborhoods. Before they became ganjapreneurs, our neighbors realized that it was better to have more brains than money. Of course, now that they have an unlimited source of capital thanks to the sacred plant, things are changing rapidly. The Einstonians recently decided to bypass the official HOA board and bring their concerns directly to the town justice. Of course, this was not necessarily a good idea.

El Sabio: "Dr. Frudito, have you ever noticed that the denizens of this community seem to take themselves too seriously?"

Dr. Freud: "Well… these eggheads are overly impressed with their own self-importance."

El Sabio: "That's right on the money, doc. They don't realize their caca stinks like everyone else's."

Dr. Freud: "Have you heard that Judge Solomon is coming to Einstein Meadows to hear some cases because he doesn't want these stoners on the road? Plus, he thinks most of them are too old to drive anyway."

El Sabio: "I never heard of a judge making house calls."

Dr. Freud: "But this isn't just any judge. Since you're indigenous to the southwest, I'm surprised you haven't heard of him. He's a descendent of the famous Judge Roy Bean."

El Sabio: "¡Ai chihuahua! You mean the hangin' judge? They're in big trouble."

Dr. Freud: "The good news is that this state no longer uses the gallows."

El Sabio: "That is good news. But I noticed the gang here built a stockade right next to the community center. And there's a big pile of rocks handy."

Dr. Freud: "*Nu?* What's wrong with a good old-fashioned stoning? But Judge Solomon is a wise one. He realizes it's better to keep all the nut jobs in one place. Everyone will be safer."

El Sabio: "This judge sounds like a piece of work. I think he's *mesheguna*."

Dr. Freud: "Since when do chihuahuas know Yiddish?"

El Sabio: "Listen, Dr. Frudito. You think humans are the only true believers? Haven't you noticed I always cover my head?" El Sabio removes his sombrero to reveal a bright red MAGA *yarmulke*.

Dr. Freud: "You might want to put your sombrero back on. You never know where those cancel culture lefties could be lurking."

El Sabio: "Speaking of locoes, I heard they still haven't found Sister Misty."

Dr. Freud: "Don't sweat it."

El Sabio: "I don't sweat nada. You're the one who's a hairy beast."

Ned walks through the ramada where Dr. Freud and El Sabio are chatting in the shade. Hearing these esteemed, local experts discuss the mental health of his neighbors, he can't resist joining the conversation.

Ned: "What neither of you know is that I heard from our in-house real estate agent that the judge was thinking about buying into Einstein Meadows last year, but changed his mind because he didn't want to be that close to the riff-raff."

El Sabio: "I can't blame him for not wanting to move into Rancho sin Saykhel."

A Case of Blind Justice –

Neighborhood Disputes Get Ugly

Although the streets in Einstein Meadows are now paved in greenish gold, we still enjoy our fair share of dilemmas.

You might be wondering why anyone would enjoy a conflict. Well, that depends on who you are. If you're a lawyer, you see gravy. If you are an aggrieved neighbor, you see red; and if you are the target of the complaint, you see potential litigation. Everyone was always disappointed when the HOA could not successfully mediate disputes, because the next step was the courts. Of course, this was the worst fear of the developer and the governing board because they did not want their dirty laundry aired in a public forum. We'll tell you about one amazing case.

Smiling Cheeks – Grease Monkey Mischief

Despite our policy differences, Brunnhilde wanted to mend some fences with us when she heard we were working on a second novel. Hoping for better treatment and a chance to show off her new patio, Brunnhilde invited

Nancy for a special sunrise St. Patrick's breakfast of Irish soda bread. Never one to deny her roots or refuse a piece of soda bread, Nancy accepted despite the early hour.

Brunnhilde: "I never get tired of this view."

Nancy: "I can see why. The sunrise light on the mountains and the desert below is spectacular. And it's so quiet."

While Brunnhilde and Nancy sip Irish Breakfast tea and munch soda bread, the trucks start to arrive. Brunnhilde had long since reconciled herself to the fact that it was not a totally unobstructed view because Filbert's house sat below hers. Fortunately, she could look over his house. And she lived at the end of the street, so there was usually very little traffic.

As she looked away from the mountains for a moment to refill the tea cups, a tow truck pulled into Filbert's driveway and unhitched an over-the-hill race car in serious need of body work. Next, the driver off-loads a huge V-8 engine.

Brunnhilde: "Drats, now I have to look at that bucket of bolts. I would love to know how that redneck ever managed to move into this neighborhood in the first place. It must have been his wife who was the brains of the outfit."

Nancy: "That's for sure. But his wife divorced him soon after they arrived here."

Brunnhilde settles back to her breakfast. Within minutes, another truck pulls up. The driver sets up some sort of contraption with chains and wheels it over to the sports car. He lays out a huge, bright blue tarp and then hoists the engine and hangs it on the chains. By this time, Brunnhilde can't take her eyes off the action below. Her tea is cold. A third truck shows up. Three guys get out and erect an awning over the engine block. That's when she goes ballistic.

Brunnhilde: "Would you look at that? The awning is totally blocking my view of the mountains and desert. Nancy, I know you're fair-minded. What do you think I should do?"

Nancy: "Well, it's pretty early, but I'd call Scott Gonzaga."

Brunnhilde calls Scott, who makes it a rule not to answer the phone before he's had a chance to gird his loins for the day's battles. So, she treks over to his house. Nancy tags along – soda bread in hand – to observe.

Brunnhilde: "Scott, my neighbor Filbert der Dorftrottel has just had a junker sports car delivered in his driveway. Another guy hoisted the engine out of it and placed an awful blue tarp on the ground. And to top it off, a third guy erected a huge awning over the sports car and engine – all of which are blocking my view. You're the developer. What are you going to do about it?"

Scott Gonzaga: (mumbling and yawning) "I'm not doing anything. It's a free country. As a matter of fact, I recall just the other day that Filbert mentioned to me he was going to start restoring an old sports car."

Brunnhilde: "Since when is he a mechanic? I thought he was a varmint control officer."

Scott: "Filbert thinks he's an expert in everything, just like the rest of you."

After she talks to Scott, Brunnhilde calls Ima on her cell phone to complain. She has forgotten Nancy, who is standing right behind her listening.

Ima: "You're up early, Brunnie. Have you spoken to Filbert yet?"

Brunnhilde: "No, I don't like to be that close to him because he always reeks of alcohol. And you know, thanks to the weed and my divinity training, those days are behind me. And, he's so obnoxious. I need a meeting scheduled pronto."

Ima: "OK, I'll set something up."

Brunnhilde: "I can't wait too long. When exactly?"

Ima: "If I really scramble, I can probably get some folks together tomorrow."

Brunnhilde: (raising her voice) "TOMORROW??!! I can't wait that long; it must be today."

Ima: (sighing): "I'll do the best I can. But I haven't had breakfast yet."

Several days go by, giving Brunnhilde more time to see Filbert out there each morning with his cheeks flashing. Filbert and Jose loudly discuss the finer points of classic junker restoration.

Brunnhilde invites Nancy back to make up for their interrupted conciliatory St. Patrick's breakfast.

Brunnhilde: "Nancy, I have to talk to someone about what's going on down there with Filbert." Although the obnoxious blue tarp and awning over the engine block wrecked Brunni's view, something darker was troubling her. "Filbert's pants slide down every time he bends over the engine, giving me an eyeful of butt cheeks. I just cannot get the thought of those hairy cheeks out of my mind, try as I might to focus on the serene landscape view. They haunt me even when I'm inside like some sort of indecent pin-the-tail-on-the-donkey game."

Nancy: "I can hear how distressed you are. I know you never had much love for Filbert, but now he's constantly mooning you."

Brunnhilde: "Exactly my point! I really must go talk to him. Scott and Ima are unwilling to address this, so as usual I have to take matters into my own hands."

Nancy and Brunnhilde walk across the street to Filbert's house.

Brunnhilde: "Excuse me Mr. der Dorftrottel! Perhaps you're not aware of it, but your awning is seriously blocking my cherished patio view."

Filbert: "I advertised myself as a good neighbor – that's how I got into the neighborhood. It's not as if I'm hanging up a laundry line across my driveway. I'll tell you what, I'll lower the height of the awning by a yard. That way, I'll still have enough headroom and your view won't be as obstructed."

> *Dear reader,*
> *As you know, Filbert is less than accommodating, so this was a huge concession for der Dorftrottel. But, Brunnhilde still was not satisfied.*

Brunnhilde hires Jose Maximilian San Carlos de Cortez, the neighborhood Jack of all trades, to put in a spiral staircase and build a deck on top of her garage so she can get a higher view. (She didn't think about the fact that this would tick off some neighbors; but she probably could care less.)

Of course, Filbert turns her into the town for building without a permit. He also files a written complaint with the Architectural Control Committee of Einstein Meadows. The town fines Brunnhilde and reassesses her property for increased living space. And the town council forces Filbert to take down his engine. (Be careful what you wish for?)

Filbert was oblivious to the fact that working on car engines in an open space of a residential neighborhood was not legal, much less considerate, but you know Filbert.

Brunnie was not a happy camper. Beyond the diminished view, the fine and the reassessment, Brunnhilde blamed Filbert for deflating her buzz. You could see daggers in Brunnhilde's eyes every time she looked at Filbert, and imagine steam pouring out of her ears.

Ultimately, Brunnhilde filed a complaint against Filbert with the police for indecent exposure. To accommodate her, the Bert decided to work naked and wear a jock strap to protect his man bits.

A deputy shows up his door to give him a summons.

Deputy Froussard: "A neighbor complained about your behavior."

Filbert: "Who is it? I have a right to face down my accuser."

Deputy: "With or without clothes?"

Filbert: "Listen, officer, this is not indecent exposure; we're allowed to go naked here."

Deputy: "Just don't show up in court like that." (He gives Fil an appearance ticket) You Einstonians are real pieces of work. Tell it to the judge."

Before the court session begins. Judge Solomon and the bailiff discuss some procedures since the hearing is occurring in a new location.

Judge Solomon: "I think we should ensure that no one has a gun handy during the deliberations. Please ask everyone to check their guns at the entrance to the ramada and give them a receipt."

Bailiff: "But judge; just about everybody in this neighborhood is naked. People only carry towels if they are going to sit down. So where could they hide guns?"

Judge Solomon: "How thoughtful and very sanitary. Who knows where those butts have been? Nevertheless, it's best to be prepared."

Bailiff: "OK. You're the boss."

A few minutes before the first case is heard ...

Bailiff: "Judge, you won't believe this. Everyone showed up wearing nothing but six guns, Stetsons, and black socks."

Dear Reader,

 Judge Solomon is blind. He is escorted into the court by his seeing-eye dog, Rusty. The judge is making a special concession to the denizens of Einstein Meadows because he learned that some of the residents are highly allergic to dogs. So instead of his usual venue at the local saloon, Judge Solomon will hear the neighborhood cases outside under the ramada (just in case you've wondered where the bar in bar association comes from.) Maybe he will take a toke instead of a drink while he's deliberating.

 The expression, 'Be careful what you wish for', may ring true for some of our neighbors since they often consider the judge's verdicts bizarre. But he does try to be fair and balanced. You will remember from the first novel that Sheriff Froussard and his deputy stopped for donuts after they captured Sister Misty, who stole the squad car to make her getaway. That donut break caused Sheriff Froussard's demotion to bailiff.

 Sadly, the judge holds Rusty the dog in higher regard than his bailiff. Whereas his great grandfather was known as the hangin' judge, Solomon is known as the baggin' judge because he likes to sentence people to his favorite insane asylum, Briarwood.

Judge: "This is truly a *fercockt* crowd. Just as well. Briarwood needs more business, and since I am a major shareholder, maybe we can bag some of these miscreants."

Bailiff: "All rise for the honorable Judge Solomon."

The judge walks in escorted by a seeing eye dog.

Judge Solomon: "I have read over the complaint against Mr. der Dorftrottel. I hear that you are a neighborhood nuisance. I wish I could see what you look like. From reading the complaint, it sounds like you are a basic redneck living among the snooty ivory-tower types at Einstein Meadows. How do you plead?"

Filbert: "Your honor, I, I, I . . ."

Judge: "I'm not finished; that was a rhetorical question. I didn't expect an answer. As for you Ms. Meiskeit, what's wrong with looking at a man's butt crack? If my eyes worked properly, I think that would be fun. However, I don't cotton to indecent exposure."

Brunnhilde had taken a series of photographs of the offending butt crack and presented them to the judge as evidence.

Judge: "I'd love to look at your photos. Next time, take Braille pictures. Then we might have something to talk about."

Filbert: "I would like a say in this matter!"

Judge: "Not in my barroom, err court. If I say you are guilty you are!"

Filbert: "Guilty of what?"

Judge: "I can't charge you for being naked in your neighborhood. But I fine you for not concealing your weapon."

Brunnhilde: "Thank you judge."

Judge: "Did I give you permission to speak. *Seked*! I am only interested in hearing myself. It was a long dusty drive and this isn't my usual air-conditioned bar. The misters on this ramada are nice, but it's not the same. By the way – where is my drink? I'm getting thirsty!"

Filbert drops his drawers to sundial the judge when he doesn't like the decision. (The judge is blind so he misses the show but he hears the laughter.)

The bailiff's dog, Rusty, goes wild and bites Filbert in the ass. Brunnhilde moons the judge. The people in the court hoot and howl.

Brunnhilde: "He can't see it anyway."

Judge Solomon: "I'm your honor to you! How many people in the audience saw that big full moon – show of hands?"

Brunnhilde: "How do you know if I have a big butt?"

Judge Solomon: "I can hear it in your voice. And, I bet you have a face that's uglier than the south end of a northbound cow."

Brunnhilde: "You can go to hell!"

Judge: "After you sweety! Arrest this bitch for disorderly conduct. I sentence you to 30 days. But first I order you to have a psychiatric evaluation at Briarwood. Take her to the funny farm. Now you don't have to worry about seeing Filbert's cute butt. Bring Filbert over here so I can feel his cheeks. Only kidding.

"Throw him out of the court room! By the way, what happened to Sister Misty? Court adjourned. Time for lunch. Via Condios!"

Nancy: (whispering to Ned) "I guess next time Brunnhilde will be extra careful what she wishes for."

> *Dear Reader, We are coming to one of our favorite epiphanies. How often does the reality of a situation not meet your expectations of it?*

CHAPTER 5-The Importance of Adjusting Your Expectations

Sometimes even groovy neighbors can become a bit too eccentric. So, with all this tumult, Nancy and I decided we needed a break from this zany enclave; and we took a six-week sail on our catamaran. While anchored by a beautiful beach off the coast of Jost van Dyke in the BVIs, we wondered what would become of our marvelous community now that the denizens had discovered the miracles of medicinal marijuana. Would our neighbors walk around in a continual state of bliss, forget to put on their clothes and create a new world order, or return to their old ways?

Then, while under the influence of some mighty fine 'Albert Einstein's Going Nuclear' custom herb, we discovered two inspiring quotes.

Nancy: "Honey, listen to what I just read. This 'Albert Einstein's Going Nuclear' is really the bomb."

Ned: "What about the quotes?"

Nancy: "Oh, yeah. The first one is: age is an issue of mind over matter. If you don't mind, it doesn't matter."

Ned: "Sounds like Mark Twain to me."

Nancy: "You're absolutely right, sweetie. However, you'll never guess who said the next one: 'There is a fountain of youth: It is your mind, your talents, the creativity you bring to life and the lives of people you love. When you learn to tap this source, you will truly have defeated age.' Any guesses?"

Ned: "Sounds great. But I give up. Who could have said that?"

Nancy: "Sophia Loren."

Ned: "Wow; what a combination. Beauty, a great brain and big bongos."

Nancy: "Honey, that sailboat is getting awfully close to us. What do you think she wants? She could be a pirate. I'll get the spear gun!"

Ned: "Wait a second; she's topless. I think we should invite her aboard. It's the only hospitable thing to do. But, first, we'll let her get a little closer to see what she has to say."

Topless Sailor: "Ahoy Nancy and Ned. I recognize you from the back cover of your amazing novel. I am so excited to meet you in person. I loved your book, and I have a copy right here. May I come aboard so you can autograph it?"

Ned: "Sure, but hang on a sec. We have a serious case of the munchies. Do you have any popcorn?"

Topless Sailor: "Of course; I wouldn't dream of visiting empty-handed."

She tosses a large backpack on the deck, climbs aboard, and pulls out a bountiful assortment of fresh fruit, top-shelf rum, cheese, and some popcorn.

Nancy: "Welcome. How wonderful to meet a fan way out here in the Caribbean! What's your name, friend?"

Topless Sailor: "It's Marguerite Ingenieux. I hope you don't mind if I drop my bikini bottom since you are both naked. I brought my own tushy towel to protect your nice leather seats."

Ned: "Great to meet you."

Nancy: "Marguerite is such a pretty name."

Marguerite: "Thanks. My mom loved it, and she always insisted people use my full name and not shorten it to Marge or Peggy."

Nancy goes below to get some refreshments and turns on the iPod; Bob Marley's "Three Little Birds" plays from the setlist.

Marguerite: "Oh, I love this song."

Nancy, Ned and Marguerite all start to sing: "Don't worry about a thing. Every little thing will be all right…"

Nancy: "Blue skies, calm water, a new friend, good tunes, and some great weed. It doesn't get much better than this." She sighs contentedly.

Ned: "Where on earth did you get all of that fresh produce so far from land?"

Marguerite: "I dumpster dive – but only outside the finest establishments. I retired when I was 21, so I could travel around the world."

Ned: "Wow, that's gutsy. What's your secret?"

Marguerite: "Besides dumpster diving, I'm an expert barterer. I paint and sell driftwood artwork, and I write a blog about my seafaring adventurers. The key is learning to adjust your expectations. I live on just $3 a day."

Nancy: "You certainly look fit, so you must eat well. By the way, who does your Brazilian waxing? Judging by the contents of your backpack, you've elevated dumpster diving to a professional endeavor. How did you acquire such a unique skill?"

Marguerite: "Actually, a mysterious older lady took me under her wing to teach me the finer points of dumpster diving – or 'encore dining' as she called it."

Ned: "I hear a good story coming. We have our own tale about dumpster diving; but you go first, Marguerite, since you are our guest. Please pass the popcorn."

Nancy: "Gosh, we're so mellow here that I forgot my manners. Marguerite, before you start the story, would you like a hit of 'Albert Einstein's Going Nuclear'? It's a custom blend that we created at Einstein Meadows."

Marguerite: "You read my mind. I'd love some, thanks." (She inhales deeply.) "I've never seen a three-foot long vape bag."

Nancy: "Besides growing our own, we also make custom vaping bags."

Marguerite: "Before I take another puff, would you mind if I stay moored here for a while so I won't be sailing under the influence? And, please remember to sign my book."

Ned: "Sure, it's our pleasure." (Ned signs Marguerite's book and passes it to Nancy who also signs it.) "Now tell us how you learned about 'encore dining'. I love that term. Kind of like leftovers meet haute cuisine. And, it sounds so much classier than dumpster diving."

Marguerite: "Well, I met this lady a few years ago when I was sailing in the Grenadines. We were both docked at a Moorings anchorage and having a drink at Pusser's bar. I was complaining about the high cost of food and supplies in the islands. Although I can't remember her name, I do remember that she claimed to have a talking horse."

Ned and Nancy smile at each other.

Marguerite: "Anyway, she told me she hadn't paid retail prices in years and survived quite well on dumpster diving. She only dove behind high-end grocery stores and fancy restaurants. In fact, later that evening, we hitchhiked into town and headed straight to one of the tonier eateries, which was getting ready to close. My mentor gracefully climbed into the dumpster and pulled out fresh garlic bread (still warm from the oven), a platter of gorgeous shrimp scampi and a full bottle of wine. We brought our haul back to the boat for a midnight feast. That was my first experience in encore dining. Of course, I don't always find such a gourmet meal; sometimes I have slim pickins'. You just never know what you'll find.

"The key is to learn how to adjust your expectations. Some days are like eating at a 5-star restaurant. Other days are slumming it at a Horn & Hardart."

Nancy: "Honey, didn't you once get tossed out of an H & H?"

Ned: "Yeah, I came with a bag lunch, but I did buy an apple and a soda."

Nancy: "That must have been in your bachelor days as a student. I'm so glad we met before some college coed snagged you."

Marguerite: (She yawns and stretches.) "That's all very interesting. Since you guys had a head start, you're obviously pretty buzzed already. Do you want me to finish the story or not?"

Ned: "Chill, Marguerite. I'm half following your tale. Too bad you can't remember your teacher's name. What did she look like?"

Marguerite: "She was very tall and skinny and had long silver hair."

Nancy: "And you said she had a talking horse?"

Ned: "Nancy, are you thinking what I'm thinking, or am I seriously stoned?"

Nancy: "You probably are stoned, honey. But she sure sounds familiar to me."

Ned whinnies.

Marguerite: "Wait. Do you know this lady? Ned, do you need a cough drop?"

Nancy: "When you first mentioned the talking horse, I began to wonder. However, when you said that she was tall and skinny with long silver hair, that clinched it. It has to be Lillian Lemishkeh."

Ned whinnies.

Marguerite: "Well, we were only on a first name basis. But Lillian does ring a bell."

Ned: "How amazing is that? Here we are far from the southwest, and we meet someone who knows one of the dumpster diving divas from Einstein Meadows."

Nancy: "Wow, you said you heard a good story coming. You weren't kidding."

Ned: "But can you believe the coincidence that Marguerite knows Lillian? What a tie-in to our own dumpster diving (aka encore dining) story."

Nancy and Ned: (sing in unison and start dancing on the deck) "It's a small world after all. It's a small world after all. It's a small world after all."

Marguerite, Nancy, and Ned: "It's a small, small world."

Marguerite: "Anyway, I'm surprised I didn't make the association from your novel. But then again, your tale of life in the desert didn't include any sailor's yarns! I do remember that woman had quite a mouth. She cursed just like a Barbary pirate. I cannot imagine how she could fit into a civilized neighborhood of scholars – let alone have earned a doctorate in anything."

Ned: "We never said she was popular. Most people just tolerated her and they found her conversations with her horse amusing. (Ned whinnies.)

"The Meadowites may once have been scholars, but they certainly haven't lost any of their passive aggressive behaviors. However, the magic weed is beginning to mellow them out. Marguerite, you may find this hard to believe, but we have our own set of dumpster diving divas. Lillian is the mastermind and the other divas are Bella Blozkop and Ava Sinnlich. We should actually call them Lillian and the Dumpster Diving Divas or the Triple D's."

The Dumpster Diving Divas of Einstein Meadows

Nancy: "Well, Marguerite do you want to hear Ned relate the story in their voices? Ned is such a good storyteller that you'll swear the divas are right here on the boat with us."

Marguerite: "Yes, Ned. Please tell the story in their voices."

Nancy brings out rum and additional munchies.

Ned: "OK, here goes. This is how we found out about the dumpster diving divas in the first place. Even though Lillian was so thin and stayed fit by riding her horse, she still worried about her weight. I told her that one of the most common consequences of becoming a kush connoisseur is serious munchies. Here's how the conversation went."

Lillian: "You're right, Ned. I get so hungry I could almost eat a cow all by myself (and I'm a vegetarian). My toking buddies and I (sorry Ned, we don't vape as you suggested at your 'Healthy Use of Marijuana Seminar') like to smoke the old-fashioned way. In fact, just the other day we were wondering how we could satisfy our almost all-consuming appetites."

Ned: "I'm sure you aging gray vixens can figure out something. You are the hottest singles on this campus."

Lillian: (sighing) "Yeah; I know what you mean! Just the other day Ava, Bella and I were fresh out of snacks after we had some doobies at my house. I told them I had an idea and went to get something out of the basement. I came back with an object no one recognized. It was very heavy and had three prongs attached to a long piece of thick rope.

"I told the gals: we will take this grappling hook, jump into the Hummer and go to the dumpster behind Trader Joe's supermarket. They close at midnight, and it's already one a.m.

Marguerite: "I know just what you're talking about, Ned. She managed to stow that hook somewhere on her boat and she brought it out when we went into town that first night. She probably got that idea from watching too many pirate movies."

Ned: "I thought I was telling this story."

Nancy: "Shhh, please. Once Ned is in the zone and weaving his story magic, it's best to let him go."

Marguerite: "Sorry, Ned. But you have to admit it's a small world and this is an amazing coincidence."

Nancy, Ned, and Marguerite: (sing in unison) "It's a small, small world."

Nancy: "This is no coincidence. It's the cosmic forces of the universe at work. Wow; that's heavy."

Ned: "OK. Where was I? Oh yeah. I told Lillian that I thought it was very dangerous to climb into a dumpster. And I asked her what sort of protective gear the divas wore. To my amazement, this is what Lillian said."

Lillian: "Who do you think we are? We are not members of the DAR. We're no wimps. I get by with cotton gardening gloves."

Ned: "Only cotton? I'd be wearing full-length leather gauntlets like the falconers use to protect themselves from the hawk's talons."

Lillian: "Oh, Ned; don't be such a party pooper. You're just upset because we didn't invite you along for the ride."

Ned: "Listen, honey; I wouldn't feel safe with you ladies in such tight quarters."

Lillian: "Don't worry Ned. We wouldn't even tempt you. Everyone knows you only have eyes for Nancy. What's more, we all know Nancy is the best shot in the neighborhood. We hear she shoots even better than you do."

Dear Reader,
You're probably wondering why the Triple Ds work so hard to find free food since we all became millionaires after we embraced ganjapreneurship. Look, just because they are not camping out at an Anti-99 Percent rally does not mean they don't enjoy getting something for nothing.

And, dear reader, you obviously haven't experienced the unique thrill of dumpster diving. I will let Lillian educate you about dumpster diving etiquette. After all, she is the dumpster diving diva of the southwest. She could probably teach you some other things. But we like to avoid censors.
Happy Nuggies!
Ned and Nancy

Ned: "The story isn't over; I just needed a break for some rum." Ned takes a sip. "So, I asked Lillian to confirm that nobody brought any gear. I told her I couldn't imagine Ava or Bella touching anything dirty."

Lillian: "Well, you are right. Ava brought a pair of surgical gloves. Bella found some chemical gloves that she uses for insecticide."

Ned: "Thank goodness you had some gear. If it was me, I would be in a hazmat suit. What about protective clothes and footwear?"

Lillian: "It's hot here in the desert. Ava wore sandals; I put on my wellies; and Bella donned her kinky hiking boots."

Marguerite: (interrupting Ned's retelling of the story again) "I think these gals are the biggest scrounges of the universe. Calling them Dumpster Diving Divas is very kind. They are back alley cats if you ask me."

Ned: "Marguerite, I'm already monged and the rum is kicking in. So, please let me finish before my train of thought totally derails."

Marguerite: (meekly) "OK. But did they ever find anything useful besides food?"

Ned: "Yes. Lillian found a vibrator that she claimed had hardly been used. So, she cleaned it up, put in new batteries, and sold it on eBay."

Marguerite: "Ewwwww! Sorry I asked. Even with all my practice adjusting my expectations, I can't wipe that gross image out of my head."

Ned: "On with the story. Honey, would you tell this part, please? My mouth is dry."

Nancy: "Sure thing, sweets. I'll pick it up where the trio asked me to come along on their next raid."

Marguerite: "Did you go?"

Nancy: "Of course, I offered to be their armed escort. You can't be too careful on that side of town in the middle of the night. And yeah, I do love my six-gun. I have the same model as Ned – mine is bigger; it's a .454 Taurus Raging Bull with a ported 7-inch barrel. It's my bear gun for grizzlies. It's so heavy that it almost requires a third arm, but I've got great biceps."

Marguerite: "You do have strong arms, Nancy. I used to have a dentist who was always admiring my upper arms." (She flexes a muscle to prove her point.)

Ned: "Hey, Marguerite; remind me to introduce you to Bella Blozkop if you're ever in our region. I think you two have a lot in common."

Nancy: "OK. Where was I? Oh, yeah. When we got out of the Hummer behind Trader Joe's, Ima Khazzer was stuck in their favorite dumpster. Ima had been stalking the divas for a long time. She was annoyed that they would not let her join the trio, and really wanted to be the fourth musketeer. The divas' refusal to bring Ima along may have been because she once teased them that she was a proud member of Mensa. Their retort was, 'We would rather be in Densa than Mensa any day'. The sad truth is that Ima just did not have the looks to hang with the Dumpster Diving Divas. Needless to say, Lillian was not happy to find Ima on her turf.

"So, here we are at the recon point, and Ima is calling out, 'Help, help. I've fallen and I'm stuck in this dumpster.' We just laughed. Not only did we have to pull Ima out, but Patsy her pet pig was also stuck. Between the two of them, it was mighty heavy lifting. Luckily, Lillian came prepared for any dumpster diving emergency. She attached a rope to the grappling iron and climbed into the dumpster with an extra rope to create a harness."

Marguerite: "That sounds like Lillian – always ready to take charge."

Nancy: "If you'll let me continue, I'll use Lillian's words to describe the scene to you."

Lillian: "How on earth did you get stuck down there, Ima?"

Ima: "Well, there was a ladder leaning against the dumpster, which I used to climb in. While Patsy and I were napping after our fine meal in the dumpster, someone took away the ladder."

Nancy: "It was quite the scene. But it gets better. Ima claimed there was a talking Chihuahua named El Sabio living in the dumpster. Can you imagine? Here's what Ima said."

Ima: "You won't believe it. Here Patsy and I are stuck for hours in this stinky dumpster in the dark. I'm whining at Patsy and asking her why she doesn't talk like Lillian's horse Trombenik. I figured if Patsy did not talk loud enough to get help, at least I would have some companionship and comfort during this trying time. Of course, I don't know if Trombenik really speaks; but Lillian claims he does. Anyway, I hear a stirring in the dumpster and things on the surface are shaking.

"My first thought was heavens, there's a rattlesnake in here. It is the southwest after all. Suddenly, a strange creature pops up. I cried out ¡ai chihuahua! And the dog says, me llamo es El Sabio. Como te llama usted? Then he started talking to me in Mexican, but I don't know the language. So, he asked me how many years I lived out west. When I told him that I had been here more than 10 years, he insulted me and said I must be one of those people who wants to build a 40-foot wall. Well, I never."

Ned: "What Ima, Lillian and the Dumpster Diving Divas didn't know is that it was Buford Swindler who took away Ima's ladder. I learned this when he showed off this incredible expanding ladder that he found at the edge of the dumpster. He told me since it was the middle of the night, he figured someone had left it there as garbage because they couldn't lift it into the dumpster. You know; finders' keepers, losers' weepers."

Marguerite: "Judging from the way you described Buford in your book, it sounds like something he would do. No doubt he billed the HOA for the new ladder. What a piece of work." Marguerite stands up and stretches.

"Ned and Nancy, that was a great story. I am so glad you invited me aboard. What a lovely afternoon. I'm going back to my hammock for a siesta."

Before Marguerite leaves, she tells us that when she returns from the Caribbean, she will embark on a new adventure to become a ganjapreneur and live off the land. Unfortunately, we forgot to ask her what she planned to do with her sailboat. Too bad, it was a sweet ride.

> *Dear Reader,*
> *We should tell you that it was Marguerite who inspired this novel. We thought that learning to adjust one's expectations is a very important skill in dumpster diving and life in general. While Marguerite didn't always find what she wanted (i.e., something tasty), she always found something she could use or something she could barter for something she needed.*

We realized we probably should head back to the southwest ourselves to see what was happening. When we left on our voyage six weeks earlier, Einstein Meadows was at build out. Perhaps, the Einstonians had finally figured out how to screen the hordes of people waiting to buy in. Maybe by now, we could see how the plan is working.

Dear Reader,
Hmmm. You probably think that Nancy and Ned are so monged that they've lost track of where the story is headed. It may look like that. However, the two wandering Einstonians retain full control of their creative faculties. Please keep reading the continuing saga. Each chapter highlights a different collective insight garnered through the wonders of ganja. This chapter was, of course, about the importance of adjusting your expectations in case you forgot.

Dear Reader, Ned and Nancy host a Seder for their neighbors. As you might expect, this was an unusual event. The interfaith group was the least surprising aspect of their Seder: The guests arrive naked; Elijah makes an appearance; and Nancy serves some powerful medicated Moses Matzoh Ball Soup. Turn the page to learn the details of this first-of-its-kind gathering.

CHAPTER 6 –

For the Unlearned, Old Age Is Winter. For the Learned, it is the Season of the Harvest – old Hasidic proverb

Ima Khazzer and Reverend Vernon Verschwender were taking a sunset walk and stopped by Ned and Nancy's adobe to say hello.

Reverend Vernon: "Hi Ned. Hi Nancy. Ima and I were wondering how your second novel is coming. Could we come in for a couple minutes? We brought some pie for dessert."

Nancy: "Sure, we'd love to have some company. But you need to tie Patsy outside on the hitching post because I'm allergic to animal dander. Plus, we keep a kosher house. Didn't you see the *mezuzah* on the door jamb?"

Ima: "My pig is short-haired and hypoallergenic. But, no problem."

Ima ties Patsy up and she and Reverend Vernon go inside.

Reverend Vernon: "So how're you doing on the second novel? Rumor has it that you're getting everybody stoned and naked."

Ned: "Well, I don't see any clothes on the two of you except for that Western-style gun holster and cowboy boots you're wearing. Could you please hang your gun holster next to mine?"

Reverend Vernon: "But I feel naked without my Colt .45."

He hangs up his six-gun. Reverend Vernon and Ima sit down.

Nancy is in the kitchen making coffee.

Ima: "Are we going to be in this novel?"

Reverend Vernon: "Of course."

Ima: "What about the rest of the Meadowites?"

Ned: "Most of them, plus a few new characters."

Nancy brings in a tray with coffee and pie.

Nancy: "Honey, don't give away too much. We should leave some room for anticipation. Let them be surprised."

Reverend Vernon: "So, what chapter are you working on now?"

Ned: "We haven't given this particular chapter a title yet; but we're trying to encourage seniors to be more open to the healing properties of medical marijuana."

Reverend Vernon: "That's a very important mission. It's so sad that members of my congregation often view life through a rearview mirror when they could be looking forward instead."

Ned: "In these trying times, it is sometimes hard to resist hiding in a cocoon."

Ima: "Well, what would encourage people to get off their *tuchis*?"

Nancy: "Ned and I were thinking about the community's upcoming trip to Amsterdam to attend the Cannabis Cup. We believe it could be more than a pursuit of money to the Einstonians. It could be an opportunity to enhance our collective cannabis education by listening to ganjapreneurs."

Dr. Freud: (appears seemingly out of thin air puffing on a cigar) "I guess you didn't realize I was listening in on your conversation. Something that has always puzzled me is that many seniors and otherwise intelligent people seem to reject the medical use of marijuana even though it could ease their pain and perhaps save their lives."

El Sabio: (suddenly appearing) "*Mazel tov*, Dr. Frudito. You're right on target. Lately, I've read promising research that marijuana is being used successfully to treat Alzheimer's patients and can prevent senility."

Reverend Vernon: "I didn't know that."

Ned: "Yes; it's true!"

Nancy: "I agree. And, Dr. Freud, please put out that stinky cigar."

Dr. Freud: "OK. But I'll have you know this is a

marijuana-infused Havana cigar and it's kosher."

Reverend Vernon: "Let's face it: many people get daffy as they get older. We need look no further than people running for public office to illustrate that point. (Note, we're not saying which candidate we're referring to.) But there are already too many folks like this in Congress who fit the description. Time for term limits!"

Ima: "It's been frustrating that I couldn't even convince some of my own family members of the benefits of medical marijuana."

Ned: "I hear you Ima. A friend of mine – a former marine no less – preferred to use WD-40 on his knees instead of the medical marijuana cream I suggested.

Reverend Vernon: "Why am I not surprised?"

Ned: "It's a pity that a lot of people rely on a biased mainstream media and ignorant and/or greedy government officials telling them what to think instead of informing themselves."

Nancy: "So in the spirit of peaceful community education, we decided to host a medicated Passover Seder this year."

Reverend Vernon: "That's great. I'll be glad to come. You know, I'm getting tired of driving across town to my brother's Seder. So, why not have one here?"

Ima: "I'd love to come too. And I'll leave Patsy at home."

Nancy: "Thank goodness!"

Reverend Vernon: "I only have one request! My brother, Rabbi Kaplan, always does the whole *megillah* in four-part harmony. Could you please find a condensed *Haggadah*? Preferably one in English so I can read it. My Hebrew is getting rusty. Latin is an easier language to remember. This way, my brother will keep it brief. As we all know, we seniors don't have very much *zitzfleisch*."

Nancy: "That's a great idea. I'll make my special matzo ball soup."

Ima: "What's special about it?"

Ned: "What do you think, Ima?"

Ima: "Oh, I get it. Nancy's soup will be medicated."

Reverend Vernon: "I like kosher food. This will be a special treat."

Ima: "My Patsy loves cannabis. Please make an extra batch of soup so I can bring it home and watch her get silly."

Reverend Vernon: "Maybe you guys could invite Brother Gunther. He's been very sad since Sister Misty was arrested and escaped."

Dr. Freud: "Oh, I think she'll be back."

There's a sniffing sound.

El Sabio: "Do I smell weed burning?"

Reverend Vernon: "I don't smell anything. You know there is an old Hassidic saying, 'For the unlearned, old age is winter. For the learned, it is the season of the harvest.' I think that's particularly relevant to seniors who could benefit from medical marijuana."

Ned: "I like that."

Nancy: "Me too. Reverend Vernon, do you mind if we use that as the title for a chapter in our new book?"

Reverend Vernon: "Go right ahead, but please give me credit. My brother, the rabbi will be impressed."

Ned: "Although neither Nancy nor I have ever taken part in a public protest, we try our best to educate people in a civil matter. When our state was getting ready to vote to legalize medical marijuana, Nancy and I designed custom tank tops to get out the vote. The text on the front of the shirt says: 'Medical Marijuana: An Intelligent Choice. Feed Your Head!' The back of the shirt says: 'Cannabis: A natural alternative to toxic medicine. Respect Your Body.'

"We wore our tank tops proudly at rock festivals all over the state and were never stopped by police or searched for weed. Not that I was worried about that. Not!! We usually received smiles and positive thumbs up. However, there were some exceptions. I remember someone sternly looking at me and saying 'You don't look sick!' I took it as a compliment, but Nancy thought I should have responded with, 'that's because I use a healthy dose of weed each day.'

"Obviously, we consider it a *mitzvah* to educate the unenlightened. But unlike missionary zealots, we use a light, humorous touch whereby we wrote our first novel: *Einstein Meadows: The Unspoken Perils and Thrills of Living in a Retirement Community.* Since our tank shirts helped the legislation to pass, we used the same company to print new shirts to advertise our first novel. This time we used the cover of our novel on one side.

"Nancy's shirt featured the book cover on the front, which made her uncomfortable when people stared at her chest to read it."

Reverend Vernon: "But it did get people to look."

Nancy: "The back said: 'Got tsuris? Dr. Freud's Rx: www.einsteinmeadows.com.' The front of Ned's shirt said 'Join the Rockin' Seniors at Einstein Meadows.' Both shirts were emblazoned with huge marijuana leaves, just to make sure everyone knew what we were about."

Our First Medicated Seder in the Buff

For those who've never attended a Seder, you're in for a real treat. We should caution you, however, that this is no ordinary Seder, and certainly not to be confused with the traditional religious observance. If you are Orthodox and easily offended, you might want to skip this section.

93

However, if you've ever been to a naked Seder, please let us know how ours compares to the one you attended; send an email to: createmiracles@einsteinmeadows.com.

Just like the Last Supper, our Seder will have a total of 13 people. If you count the number of guests as they arrive, you will realize that one person is missing. That is because there is always one seat left empty for the prophet Elijah. But tonight, you're in for a treat because Elijah actually shows up. The question you must ask yourself is … "Will he be naked?"

The Seder was a potluck dinner; everyone volunteered to bring traditional dishes for the meal.

Rabbi Kaplan will be co-hosting this medicated Seder with Dr. Freud. Rabbi Kaplan greets the guests as they arrive at Ned and Nancy's new villa. Dr. Freud announces everyone as he escorts each guest into the large dining room while Bob Marley's song "Exodus" plays in the background. Dr. Freud is naked as are all the guests. But, being Freud, he kept on his black bow tie and black socks. He smokes a peace pipe filled with marijuana.

The first guests to show up are Ima Khazzer and Reverend Vernon Verschwender. Ima was still a little peeved that she had to leave her prized pet pig Patsy at home. But she came prepared with a bucket for leftovers to bring Patsy. She was excited because this was to be her first Passover Seder and she had never eaten any kosher food. Reverend Vernon gives his brother Rabbi Kaplan a big hug. He had never missed one of his brother's Seders, and he was excited that Dr. Freud would co-host the event this year. He wondered if Dr. Freud would psychoanalyze the guests. What do you think?

Dr. Freud: "Ms. Ima Khazzer and Reverend Vernon Verschwender. That's a very aromatic brisket you've brought, Ima. Thanks for bringing a case of Manishevitz, Reverend."

Ima: "As-salamu alaykum."

Reverend Vernon: "By the way, Ima, you should be aware that you used the Arabic greeting. Jews say *shalom aleichem.* But," (adding in a gentle voice), "I know your intentions were good."

Dr. Freud: "Looks like we'll all be getting *shikkered* tonight. I mean plastered. But unfortunately, we can't open the wine until we start the Seder."

Reverend Vernon: "Hey, Doc; I know the rules. Rabbi Kaplan is my brother."

Zachariah Denker and Chief El Guappo arrive next.

Chief El Guappo: "*Pesach Sameach!*"

Rabbi Kaplan: "I didn't know there were Jewish Apaches."

Dr. Freud: "Shalom."

Chief El Guappo holds out a freshly killed and cooked wild turkey.

Dr. Freud: "That bird is way too big for me to handle. *Oy*, I've got a hernia. Please just put it on the table, Chief. Where on earth did you find such a huge turkey?"

Chief El Guappo: "We're Apaches. We hunt for our food as we always have."

Dr. Freud announces Zachariah Denker. Zachariah places a festive fruit basket on the Seder table.

Dr. Freud: "Lillian Lemishkeh, Bella Blozkop and Ms. Lilith. My, you ladies look particularly fetching tonight. Bella, that sorbet looks lickable. Thanks for the chocolate macaroons Lilith; they're Nancy's favorite. Lillian, what can I say? Hard-boiled eggs – very practical."

Dr. Freud: "Dr. Ray Rising Sun." (Ray brings a bunch of manzanas.) "I gotta' try those poco pangas. At last, we'll resolve the age-old question: does size matter?"

Ima: "Just ask your favorite Congressman."

Dr. Freud: "What does that have to do with anything?"

Ima: "They're all wieners."

Dr. Ray Rising Sun: (wears a custom embroidered *yarmulke*) "Shalom."

Rabbi Kaplan: (looks a little surprised by Ray's greeting) "*Pesach Sameach.*"

Dr. Freud: "Vas is dos? We got more Native American Jews here than Ashkenazi."

Rabbi Kaplan: "Naturally. This is the West."

Nancy and Ned seat their guests at the large table.

Bella: "Why is there an empty seat next to me? I'm used to being a third wheel, but I didn't expect to be insulted at my first Seder."

Nancy: "It's for Elijah."

Bella: "Who is he?"

Nancy: "We don't know. You never know who will show up."

Bella: "I hope he's tall, dark and handsome."

Rabbi Kaplan provides an orientation for the traditional reading of the *Haggadah*, the prayer book that includes the rituals for the Passover Seder. Nancy and Ned give a copy of the prayer book to each guest.

Reverend Vernon: "Thank goodness, it's in English."

Nancy: "Of course. We're hosting an ecumenical Seder and we want everyone to feel included."

Chief El Guappo: "What kind of *fercockt* version is this? Nobody here reads Hebrew."

Rabbi Kaplan: "As Nancy explained, we are trying to be inclusive here. Not everyone is as classically trained as you are Chief."

Chief El Guappo: "None the less, you are all welcome to

come to Sunday school on the reservation. It's never too late to learn your ancestral language. And the only way to keep the language and culture alive is to stay fluent."

Each person around the table takes a turn reading a section from the *Haggadah*.

Bella: "I forgot my reading glasses. Ima, would you please read my section?"

The Passover Seder continues with some of the ritual prayers.

Rabbi Kaplan: "Nancy, would you please read the four questions?"

Nancy: "Why me? Traditionally, it's the youngest boy who reads the questions."

Rabbi Kaplan: "You're the youngest person here since you're 20 years younger than Ned."

Dr. Freud: (turning to Ned) "You did well my son."

Nancy: "Fine; I'll be honored to read them. Gee, this reminds me of my very first Seder, which was also when I met Ned's family for the first time. Ned's father assigned this task to me."

Ned: "You did fine, honey. I never had any doubts about you at your first Seder. And, of course you handled my family with grace."

When we get to the retelling of the four plagues that befell the Egyptians as punishment for enslaving the

Jews, Dr. Freud leads the group in a conga line around the dining room singing *Dayenu*.

As the guests are about to drink the third glass of ritual wine, Ned opens the door so Elijah can enter. Another custom is that when the doors are open, a poor person may come inside and join the family for a feast.

Nancy: "We're going to add a creative twist to our first Seder here. What if Elijah came in a different form? For instance, the Pope, Abraham Lincoln, Mahatma Gandhi, or Mark Twain? What would his initial comments be?"

Ned: "If the Pope shows up, he'll be speaking Hebrew."

Chief El Guappo: "With Gandhi, at least we've got one more Indian to break up all those old white guys, even if he's not a Native American."

Ray: "You got that right, Chief."

Lillian Lemishkeh: "Mark Twain was my favorite childhood author. He'll bring some humor to this event."

Reverend Vernon: "I don't know if Lincoln will be able to fit in the door. If he doesn't hit his head on the way in, hopefully he'll bean himself on the way out."

Nancy: "Spoken like a true Southerner."

Reverend Vernon: "As I always say, the South will rise again."

A familiar voice calls through the front door.

Visitor: "Is anyone home?" Everyone immediately

recognizes the visitor. It's Jose Maximillian San Carlos de Cortez, the neighborhood handyman. He's fully naked, but sports a red MAGA baseball hat.

Rabbi Kaplan: "If you don't mind, could you please take off your baseball cap? We have a spare *yarmulke*."

Jose: "That won't be necessary." He takes off his hat to reveal a bright red yarmulke with Hebrew lettering of someone's name and the numbers 2020. (Can you guess which name?)

Bella: "I almost didn't recognize you without your clothes and tool belt. What brings you here?"

Jose: "The smell of delicious cooking is wafting for miles. So, I followed my nose and here I am."

Bella: "There's a seat right next to me. I've been waiting for you. Next time you do work at my house, why don't you show up naked? I always appreciate a well-hung man."

Rabbi Kaplan: "Let's try to maintain a little decorum. Even though we're all naked, this is still a religious observance. Show some respect."

Dr. Freud: "Yah. Keep your id in your pants."

Bella: "What pants? I have a bare bottom just like everyone else."

Chief El Guappo: "*Oy vey.*" As he shakes his head, the feathers on his headdress dance.

Reverend Vernon: "We got some hot tickets in this crowd."

Zachariah Denker: "Gee, Jose, I didn't know you were Jewish. How come you keep it a secret?"

Jose: "With all the Germans in the Meadows, I didn't know if it was a good idea to come out publicly. I learned that the bund met in the last neighborhood I worked in before and during World War II."

Ima: "I'm getting hungry. Where's the main deal? There's only so much matzo you can have, and I think it's giving me gas."

Everyone at the table wrinkles their noses: "We noticed."

Chief El Guappo: "Wait until we get to the turkey."

Then it is time to enjoy the meal. The first dish is Nancy's magic matzo balls.

Nancy: "I have added the secret ingredient that has been lost across the centuries of time. Since this is a religious observance, I added cannabis-infused oil from the sacred plant."

Of course, Nancy knew that the guests attending the Seder all lived in the community, so no one had to drive. This is a good thing because after the first round of uncontrollable giggles, the matzo balls have been known to put people to sleep for a solid nine hours. We deduced that this is obviously how the ancient Jews escaped their Egyptian captors. The Israelites got a huge head start while the guards slept. Of course, the parting of the red sea was God's handiwork. All Moses did was stir the pot.

Dear Reader,
We know you may be skeptical. But the fact is that marijuana seeds were found in sealed Egyptian tombs. So, there is no reason to doubt the veracity of the story.
Nevertheless, the recipe works. Unfortunately, due to the vagaries of US law and the dim-witted light bulbs who occupy Congress, we cannot give you the precise proportions. If you are fortunate enough to live in a state where medical or recreational marijuana is legal, you should be able to figure it out for yourself. But beware; dosing marijuana in edibles can be very tricky. We suggest reading The Cannabis Gourmet Cookbook, *by Cheri Sicard (aka Cannabis Cheri).*

Everyone enjoyed a sumptuous feast. As we ate dessert, Dr. Freud took out a large brown bag.

Dr. Freud: "Reach into the bag without looking and take out an object. Then share how you think the object fits into the Passover story."

Bella pulls out a bright yellow tennis ball.

Bella: "You don't have to be Jewish to know this one. The Jews have been bounced around from country to country for centuries."

Dr. Freud: "Hmmm."

Reverend Vernon: "I knew you'd be up to your old tricks, Doc."

Reverend Vernon takes a bar of soap out of the bag.

Reverend Vernon: "Oh, my mom's favorite way to discipline."

Rabbi Kaplan: "Yeah, bro, I think Mom always thought you were the wicked son."

Ms. Lilith: "Now this is getting interesting. How can we have two brothers representing the clergy from different religions?"

Nancy: (interrupts) "We'll have no airing of family business during this celebration. How do you think the soap fits into the Passover story?"

Reverend Vernon: "Well, haven't you been paying attention? The Seder includes ritual washing of hands. Soap comes in real handy."

Dr: Freud: "Lilith, it's your turn. Take something out of the bag."

Lilith pulls out a light bulb, which mysteriously lights up when she touches it.

Lillian: "What's with that?"

Ms. Lilith (with a sly smile): "The Jews found their way out of the darkness through their Exodus and we celebrate that at Passover."

Everyone gets so blitzed that they fall asleep at the table during dessert. They wake up the next morning because they have the ravenous munchies without knowing they slept the whole night. At our Seder, everyone ate reclining just like the ancient Jews did, so it was no problem that our guests crashed. Nancy had wisely included pillows on people's seats at the start of the meal, and taken everything off the stove in advance. Safety First!

Dear Reader,
Pack your bags and get ready to fly. Two groups
of Einstonians are about to travel to Amsterdam
for a truly educational and life-altering
experience. And they don't even need continuing
educational credits.

CHAPTER 7 -

"Just Remember: When You're Over the Hill, You Begin to Pick Up Speed"

– Charles Schultz

Imagine a person in a wheelchair flying down the hill. The person is wearing a Chinese flying cap and airman goggles, plus a Snoopy- style fringed red scarf billowing in the breeze.

We recognize that all different age groups read our novels, and possibly some teens without parental permission. Those of you who are seniors like us already realize that time seems to pass faster the older we get. So, there's no time to waste. Keeping that in mind, several very enthusiastic neighbors volunteered to go on a joint field trip to attend the International Congress on Love and Sex with Robots and the Cannabis Cup.

The Einstonians wisely realize this is the best time to travel since our energy levels are diminishing quicker than we would like. And, they seize the once-in-a-lifetime opportunity that the Congress on Love and Sex with Robots and the Cannabis Cup are scheduled simultaneously in Amsterdam. That's kismet!

Brunnhilde Meeskeit: (addressing the 16 other volunteers in the Ponderosa Room) "Well, the time has come to prepare for our two field trips to Europe. You'll be happy to know there will be seats available for some of your private butlers and maids. I did that for you Ned and Nancy; I know you don't go anywhere without Yo, James." **Ms. Lilith:** (winking at Nancy) "It's nice to have a man servant."

Brunnhilde: "You may also be wondering why Barry, Leopold's pet chimp, and Lilith's Pomeranian, Wilfred, are here. Leopold and Lilith begged me to allow their service animals to come. I know some of you have allergies to pet dander, so the animals will fly in the back of the plane. Since the private jet we've hired has the bathrooms up front, that shouldn't present a problem for Nancy and Ned."

Dr. Freud: "What sort of *bupkes* is this? Ever since the ADA was modified to include *mesheguna* dogs . . . (he sneezes loudly) . . . I've been appalled for what passes for psychiatric judgment these days. With all due respect Lilith and Leopold, I think you both need to get yourselves into real therapy. The idea that animals could be a substitute for therapy is pure poop!"

Lilith (stands up to speak): "Listen, you crazy old coot. Get with the program!"

Leopold Spieber: (jumps up): "Yeah, times have changed."

Ava Sinnlich: "How do you plan to get Barry into the hotel?"

Leopold: "I'm going to sneak Barry into the hotel by disguising him as a baby and putting him in a carriage. And now that you mention it, Ava, you can wheel him in. The staff will be too busy looking at you to notice my hairy chimp with his bottle."

Ava: "You better lighten up his face because we are not black."

Leopold: "Not a problem. I'll just lather him up with Coppertone zinc cream. He will look like Count Chocula."

Siegfried Zynismus: "Better not let the BLM folks hear you say that."

Ava: "What about you Lilith, what are you going to do about Wilfred?"

Lilith: "That's easy. He is a special-needs dog; so, I'll just put on his bright red MAGA vest and carry my therapy dog ID. I'll make sure I have proof of all his vaccinations."

Brunnhilde: "We have business to discuss. I have already settled the animal issue myself; so, let's move on.

"We will separate our volunteers into two teams for this exploratory investment adventure. The teams will be charged with keeping detailed notes so they can come back and report to the investment club."

Heckler: "Homework. What a surprise!"

Brunnhilde: "Not to worry. You'll still have plenty of time to network and explore the offerings of both conferences. Our neighbors who are staying home are funding this trip, and they expect to be kept in the loop. Buford and I have decided who will be on each team."

Buford Swindler: "We based the team's makeup on the interest each of you has previously shown in these two topics. Since we're all staying at the same hotel, we'll be able to compare notes."

> *Dear Reader,*
> *As our sophisticated audience probably knows, the International Congress on Love and Sex with Robots provides an "excellent opportunity for academics, artists, and industry professionals to discuss and present their work."*
> *The Cannabis Cup is the world's largest cannabis experience that includes seed companies, growers, and all kinds of accessory products for the weed connoisseur. The Cannabis Cup recognizes and awards the best cannabis products available. The best strains will be honored. Take out your notebooks!*

Professor Growmore: "We want to learn more about growing and hybridizing and to research how to compete in the future. We know we have the best shit, but we're still refining our crop. As retired academics, we want to be sure we get it right before we compete in the big leagues."

Filbert der Dorftrottel: "I may not be an ivory tower egghead, but I am certainly a Road Scholar and know a good piece of ass when I see it. I assume Brunnhilde made the right choice about which conference I should attend."

Brunnhilde: "OK, OK; I'll share the list." (She turns on an overhead projector with a chart of the teams.)

Amsterdam Field Trip Teams

(Kinkhounds)

Love and Sex with Robots:
* Ben

* Bella

* Ava

* Siegfried

* Dr. Jeannette

* Filbert

* Lillian

* Dr. Quackenbush

Amsterdam Field Trip Teams

(Stoners)

Cannabis Cup:
* Professor Growmore

* Nancy and Ned

* Buford

* Leopold

* Brunnhilde

* Zachariah

* Dr. Coconut

* Lilith

Ava: "What about the room assignments?"

Brunnhilde: "Oh! I almost forgot. Gee, my memory is nearly as bad as that guy who was hiding in his basement bunker while running for office."

Siegfried: "Now, now. We don't need any political commentary."

Filbert: "Why not? He seems to have stolen the election."

Brunnhilde: "Come on people. Let's stay on topic, please. I've assigned rooms by the gender you were born. Of course, Ned and Nancy will share a room together."

Bella Blozkop: "You mean I can't share a room with Ben?"

Brunnhilde: "I'm not even going to dignify that with a response."

Bella: (with a wink) "We'll see about that."

Ava: "You little minx."

Brunnhilde: "Ben and Filbert will share a room."

Filbert: "He snores!"

Ben Chardonnay: "No, I don't!"

Bella: "Yes you do!"

Brunnhilde: "There will be no dirty laundry aired today."

Bella: "I think snoring is cute."

Ben: "Well you snore too."

Brunnhilde: "Bella and Ava will share a room, Dr. Jeannette and Lillian, Siegfried and Dr. Quackenbush.

Lilith will share a room with me because I'm not allergic to dogs. Dr. Coconut and Buford. Professor Growmore and Zachariah.

"Now it's time to split into our two respective teams. You need to figure out who will be the team leaders and who will be the secretary to take detailed notes. Remember: we must present to the community when we return. Even though we're retired, we don't want to look like *schleppers* in front of our peers."

Dr. Freud: "Or *schlemiels.*"

Sex with Robots Team

Let's listen in on the Love and Sex with Robots team (aka Kinkhounds) as they attempt to get organized.

Ben: "Well, as you all know I make frequent presentations on cruise ships and I'm very comfortable with public speaking so that when we come back to Einstein Meadows, it will be easy for me to present our findings to our colleagues, I mean neighbors."

Bella and Ava (simultaneously): "Oh, you're so right, Ben."

Dr. Quackenbush: "Listen, as a physician, you will need my expertise because we have to be concerned about foreign bodies and disease."

Jeannette Gedankenlos: "Hold on Quack! As a psychologist, I'm concerned about the ethical and moral implications that you MDs frequently overlook."

Filbert: "Time to cut the horseshit. Let's get serious."

Lillian Lemishkeh: "I don't like anyone insulting horses – especially my Hansie."

Filbert: "We all know why you like Hansie – because he's hung like a stallion."

Lillian (exasperated): "Duh; he is a horse."

Siegfried: "Enough of this squabbling. I think Ben should lead the group and co-chair it with Dr. Quackenbush. Dr. Jeannette can be the scribe."

Filbert: "I second that. Everyone agree?"

The group unanimously consents.

Ben: "Finally, we can get down to business. Brunnhilde wisely gave me a copy of the entire symposium schedule. So, we can decide who will go to which lecture."

Filbert: "Oh, I see the fix is already in. How'd she know you were going to be the leader? If there's anything about marrying a robot, count me in. Since I haven't had luck in this area, I might as well find something that will follow my every command and be able to satisfy me. After all, I am a real man."

Lillian (in an aside): "He sure knows how to dish it out."

Ben: First I'd like to recommend that you watch *Lars and the Real Girl* (2007); it's currently on Amazon Prime. It will set the stage for what we might hear. Here are some of our choices:

*Lying Cheating Robots: Robots and Infidelity
Ben: "Bella and I will take that one! Don't worry there are plenty more topics available, including sessions on robot emotions, personalities, etc."

*Reflections on Moral Challenges Posed by a Childlike Sexbot
Ava: "I like that one!"

*Advantages and Disadvantages of Sex with Robots
Siegfried: "Now, that sounds like a thinking man's choice."

*Coolest Robots to Have Sex with Today
Bella: "Me, I want that one!"

*Why Not Marry a Robot?
Filbert: "Now we're talking."

*Love Doll Rental: Perils and Pitfalls
Filbert: I'll take that too!"

*Sex Robots and Ethical Issues
Jeannette: "That's got my name on it."

*Robots as Girlfriends and Mistresses

Ben: "Obviously, that's mine."

*Intimacy with Robots – a Psychoanalytical Perspective

Dr. Quackenbush: "Sounds good to me."

*Will Sexbots Replace Sex Workers?

Siegfried: "I've got that covered."

*Where do We Draw the Line? A Religious Perspective on Sex with a Robot

Lillian: "I was praying for something spiritual."

Ben: "See; that wasn't so hard."

Filbert: "I hope there will be plenty of breaks to smoke and drink and try out the goods."

Cannabis Cup Team Gets the Heads Up

Meanwhile on the other side of the room, the Stoners – or the Cannabis Cup team to be politically correct – put their heads together.

Professor Growmore: "While our kinkier colleagues will be stuck in stuffy conference rooms all day at the Love and Sex with Robots conference, we will be out on the town experiencing all the wonderful weed opportunities that Amsterdam has to offer."

Ms. Lilith: (looking around) "I see that Brunnhilde and Buford knew who the real ganja connoisseurs and party animals were. This is going to be fantastic. I can't wait."

Brunnhilde: "Thanks for that Lilith. I've lived with these folks long enough to know who I want to hang with."

Zachariah Denker: "Just remember. Marijuana is technically not legal in Amsterdam. It has simply been decriminalized. The cops tolerate weed use so they can concentrate on addictive drugs."

Professor Growmore: "That's right, Zach. And as some of you probably know, the Cannabis Cup is more of a festival than a symposium. The field testing takes place in coffeeshops all over the city."

Nancy: "With so many choices, how will we know which shops to visit?"

Lillian: "Good question, Nancy. I found a great resource to all things cannabis in Amsterdam including maps, coffeeshop etiquette and whose got what. *The Smoker's Guide* is specifically geared toward tourists and visitors. I ordered several copies for the library, and brought them today. Also check out www.smokersguide.com for the most up to date info."

Professor Growmore: "That's perfect, Lillian. Why don't you guys check it out? Then we can plan our visit."

Ned: "The great thing about the Cannabis Cup is that we won't be tied to a schedule. The cannabis scene is pretty much 24/7 in Amsterdam. And to get the party started, musicians provide live entertainment right in the exhibition hall."

Leopold: "All right. Time to party on."

The Plane Ride: Wild Times in the Sky?

Our two teams drove the Woodstock bus to the airport. Naturally, as we drove through town, the electric loudspeakers mounted to the roof of the bus blared "Woodstock", by Crosby, Stills, Nash and Young. The Meadowites enjoyed the attention as people on the street waved and gave thumbs up for the community's collective work of art and joie de vivre.

As we prepared for takeoff, our pilot popped in a CD with Bob Dylan's "Rainy Day Woman #12 and 35".

Everyone sings the chorus with gusto: "But, I would not feel so all alone, everybody must get stoned!"

Luckily, Leopold and Lilith medicated their pets for the flight, and the animals slept soundly; Baked Biscuit was the perfect choice for Wilfred. And, we whizzed through the private security area. Five Benjamins go a long way at the airport. However, after the eight-hour transatlantic flight, the meds wore off. Barry was consumed by crazy munchies and Wilfred barked uncontrollably. Fortunately, Dr. Coconut came prepared with tranquilizers. He gave the animals their injections so expertly you would have thought he was a veterinarian. This calmed Barry and Wilfred right down and we cleared customs in Holland without incident.

Who Has Never Been Thrown Out of a Hotel?

If you've never been thrown out of a hotel, you haven't experienced life on the wild side. When you get to be a senior, it's time to let your hair down and be free.

Dear Reader,

My grandfather used to tell my mom he would bring me back a pet monkey from Florida. I think my mother lived in fear that he might really bring me a monkey. Instead, he used to send me post cards with a monkey playing guitar, driving a red sports car, etc. He did bring me back a baby stuffed alligator with razor sharp yellowed teeth that I kept on my desk throughout childhood and college. However, in retrospect my mom was right about monkeys creating mayhem and wrecking rooms. Wait until you read what happened. . .

Now the Bad News

OK, the Einstonians managed to sneak Barry into the hotel. As Leopold predicted, everyone was distracted by Ava's voluptuous body as she wheeled Barry in a baby carriage. Plus, Wilfred stayed calm in Lilith's arms. However, the peace was short-lived.

When the chambermaid came in to clean the room, Leopold was taking a shower. Barry scooted out the open door into the hallway while the chambermaid changed the sheets. A fierce case of the munchies made Barry desperate to find something to eat. Ned was riding in the elevator and the operator asked him if he would wait while he took a quick stroll down the hallway to investigate a skunky smell. He put the elevator on hold. Faster than you can say "Holy cheetah," Barry jumped in when the doors opened and grabbed the operator's cap. The surprised operator tried to keep the doors from closing. Barry flips the switch and takes a seat on the operator's stool; and gives Ned a knowing wink.

Now, I haven't shared this yet, but Barry can use sign language, understands some basic English, and can read numbers. Leopold has taught him well. Other guests are startled as they enter the elevator.

Ned: "Just tell him what floor you want."

To everyone's amazement, Barry presses the correct floor. Mind you this is a 13-story hotel and chimpanzees get bored easily. Barry starts pressing all the buttons. The people in the elevator get annoyed and just get out when the doors finally open, loudly exclaiming that this chimp is a nut job.

Nancy noticed the elevator was going up and down while she was waiting for Ned in the lobby. When the elevator finally comes to a stop in the lobby, Barry runs out. He swings from the chandeliers, creating mayhem. Barry flies through the room, scratching people, and pooping all over. The hotel staff desperately tries to catch him and figure out to whom he belongs.

Since he's so hungry, Barry follows his nose to a banquet hall with a buffet set out. He jumps all over the buffet table, grabbing bananas, shoving cake into his mouth. He guzzles a long drink from the champagne fountain.

When Leopold comes down and sees Barry behaving wildly, he blows a loud whistle. Barry stops dead in his tracks and sheepishly scrambles over to Leopold.

Leopold wags his finger at Barry.

Leopold: (in a scolding voice) "Barry! Oh, Barry! What have you done?"

At that point the hotel manager realizes Barry belongs to Leopold.

Hotel manager: "You and your entourage of Meadowites are banished from coming to this hotel forever. How did you think you would be able to smuggle a chimpanzee into a hotel? What a mess!"

Chambermaid: "You should see the room upstairs. Or maybe you shouldn't unless you have a strong stomach. And the SMELL!"

Filbert: "That's OK. Are there any other Hiltons in this town?"

Hotel manager: "You bourgeois Americans are all alike. Get out of my hotel. But first you must settle the bill. Who's the financier of this group?"

Filbert: "That would be Buford. He's upstairs in his room getting ready for dinner."

Chambermaid: "Make sure you charge them extra to cover the tip they forgot to leave for me."

Buford settles the bill and out the door we go. The hotel staff was so anxious to see us leave that they threw our luggage out on the street behind us. Buford gave the hotel manager a huge bribe so he wouldn't call the nearby hotels to blacklist us.

Buford: "I'm not happy with you idiots. How am I going to explain the extra charges when we get back to the Meadows?"

Ava and Bella: (in unison) "Don't worry dear; you'll figure it out."

Buford: "OK. But you need to get your acts together. And, get a move on. We must find another hotel before word gets out about our group."

Wearing a bright red MAGA therapy vest, Wilfred pees on several people in the street as the group walks to their next hotel.

Do you think the shenanigans will stop? Don't bet on it. The Kinkhounds were on their best behavior during the International Congress of Love and Sex with Robots. They enjoyed meeting other folks with similar eccentricities. The Congress attendees were amused that seniors from an investment club wanted to include sex robots in their portfolios as well as buy some for themselves.

The weed hounds at the Cannabis Cup shared many a toke with the senior stoners and liked the idea that the Einstonians lived in a sexually liberated neighborhood. Everyone exchanged emails and phone numbers because the Cannabis Cup group wanted to visit to experience this American Shamballa themselves. For those of you who have attended professional conferences, you know it's not just about the educational sessions. The behind-the-scenes networking is just as important – and often more memorable.

After Buford read the group the riot act, everyone behaved like model citizens. With the two big events in town the same week, hotel rooms were very scarce and the group could not risk being thrown out of a second hotel.

The Stoners and Kinkhounds gather lots of information. And, as former academentians, they take copious notes. But this group loves to party.

Jeannette and Lillian hire two male escorts, then have the nerve to put it on their expense sheets. Not to be outdone, Filbert and Ben run up a $1,000 tab for the mini bar, which Filbert thought was on the house. Filbert was arrested for trying to have a quickie with a sex robot on the convention floor.

Bella and Ava hire a male stripper. But the last straw is when they try to use their strap-ons and the escorts call the police. Of course, the ladies get arrested and Buford reluctantly bails them out. Buford threatens them with the stockade when they get back to Einstein Meadows.

Professor Growmore and Dr. Coconut try out too many free samples and literally go up in smoke. Lilith's test pup Wilfred gives new meaning to getting monged. He has a psychedelic freak-out and tries to hump everyone's leg while peeing all over the place.

Meanwhile Barry loves the ganja and starts extolling the virtues of the different strains. Who knew chimps could talk so eloquently? Maybe he will run for public office someday. Yeah, when the moon turns green.

Of course, Ned and Nancy stay out of trouble. And the two boy scouts Dr. Quackenbush and Zachariah don't stir the pot; they just smoke it. However, they did share with Ned that they hooked up with a pair of leather-clad nympho grannies. Let's hope they don't invite them to visit the Meadows. Your guess is as good as mine.

Everyone on the Stoner team shares an 8-foot-long volcano bag just like the one we described in our first novel.

Brunnhilde: "OK, my fellow academentians. It's time to get ready for our trip home. I want everybody to start thinking about how we are going to present our findings to the rest of the community at Einstein Meadows when we return. I'm sure they are anxiously awaiting our findings."

Filbert: "Can we share all of our misadventures with the folks back home?"

Buford: "Absolutely not! They are already think you are all degenerates; we don't want to confirm their biases."

Ava: "We don't want to give away our secrets. Remember: what happens in Amsterdam stays in Amsterdam."

Ben: "Wow; we have a lot to think about. I suggest everyone buy a pad at the airport so you can jot down your thoughts instead of napping on the plane."

Dear Reader, I think it's reasonable to assume that the Einstonians may be over the hill, but they are still on top of their skis. Turn the page and see what happens when they present their findings to the community.

CHAPTER 8 -

Progress Not Perfection

The Einstonians eagerly await the presentations on the Cannabis Cup and International Congress of Love and Sex with Robots. 'Chariots of Fire' plays as people enter the auditorium.

Brunnhilde Meeskeit: (standing by podium) Ben and Professor Growmore are seated next to her to talk about their findings.

"Wow, this is the largest turnout we've ever had. Today we will hear from our two Amsterdam teams – the Kinkhounds and the Stoners. Up first is the Love and Sex with Robots committee chaired by Ben Chardonnay. Then the stoners committee chaired by our own Professor Growmore will share their experiences at the Cannabis Cup."

Thunderous applause and whistles

Ben Chardonnay: "Welcome my fellow academentians. Excuse me, I meant academics. Ned's got me totally confused ever since he introduced the other word. But you know how it is. As we get older, our minds play tricks on us. First, I'm happy to say that this was a really productive trip. And we didn't even get into too much trouble."

Ava Sinnlich: "Shhh Ben; gentlemen don't kiss and tell."

Ben: "We met many interesting people, and we invited some folks to visit us here at the Meadows. Even though we don't have any more houses available, we thought our new like-minded friends would enjoy a tour of our clothing-optional neighborhood. Everybody wants a ride in our Woodstock bus.

And, a major, formerly great newspaper invited us to be subjects of an article in their Sunday magazine. You'll be happy to hear that we declined since we didn't want to be associated with that left-wing rag. Instead, *Rolling Stone* and *High Times* magazines will feature us in cover stories. But that's enough meandering. Let's get right to the point. Filbert, would you raise your hand please?"

Filbert der Dorftrottel: "Here I am, Ben." (Filbert is seated way in the back in the far-left corner of the room).

Ben: "Fil, would you be so kind as to introduce your special guest?"

Filbert: "Delilah, please stand and curtsy for our friends."

Delilah: (with a heavy Southern drawl) "Pleased to meet y'all."

Scott Gonzaga: "Wow, Filbert; she's a knockout."

Delilah: "Yes, I know. What's your name, big boy? I can handle more than one at a time."

Filbert: "Hold on a sec, Delilah. I thought you were my one and only."

Ben: "Our group concluded that sex robots are the wave of the future. Delilah accompanied us on the way home; but with Buford's approval, we ordered two more to take advantage of the steep vendor's discount we were offered."

Heckler: "It's time for Sister Misty to return. This neighborhood is going to hell!"

Buford Swindler: "Far be it from me to turn down such a bargain. Subject to a community vote, of course, we'd like to invest $250,000 in the company that invented Delilah with some of the profits from our cash crop. That's the Roxxxy from TrueCompanion that Ned suggested at our investment club meeting last year. We were lucky enough to get a private demonstration in Amsterdam.

"We assume that investment will grow to several million dollars in the next decade. Why should we settle for being in the top one percent, when we are heading toward being in the top one-tenth of one percent? Does anyone in the audience have any questions?"

Ima raises her hand. Ben walks over to Ima and hands her the wireless microphone.

Ima Khazzer: "Did anyone check out the electronic kissing machine?"

Bella Blozkop: "Yes, I did. The Kissenger machine allows couples to blow kisses long distance. Ima, I know Patsy likes to kiss you. Now she can send swiny kisses to all your friends and relatives."

Ima: "Plus, it's a great way to screen potential dates."

Cara Chasid: "What about the interactive sex toys they had last year? I'm sure they were on display again."

Ms. Lilith: "Of course; I played with some of them."

Cara: "Were they as good as I dreamt about?"

Lilith: "Actually they were better."

Dr. Freud: "How do you know what she dreamt about? I'm the only one qualified to do dream analysis."

El Sabio: "That's what you think, doc."

Siegfried Zynismus: "I'm still not sure about this investing in sex robots. I don't think we should be indulging people's baser instincts. I would love to know what Sister Misty would say about this."

Brunnhilde: "You know Sister Misty is no longer with us. Show some respect for our absent, but not forgotten member of the clergy."

Brother Gunther Shaygetz: "She'll be back and you'll find out soon enough what she thinks. She's pretty kinky, but I'm not sure she would approve."

Dr. Freud: "Automatons would do a world of good, especially for people who don't fit the so-called 'normal' mode. For example, those who experience lots of rejection or all those professors with Asperger's syndrome."

Bella: "With all due respect to Dr. Freud and Filbert, I'm not sure about this idea of sex with robots because sex dolls objectify women. Dr. Freud, have you forgotten your earlier theories? I thought you believed that an uncontrolled id is always a bad idea. That's why we have a super ego. Don't you think therapy would be a better option for people who have trouble with interpersonal relationships?"

Dr. Freud: "Times change and theories can evolve, my dear. I'd love to find a woman who doesn't object to my cigar breath or to my wearing black socks during sex. Some people desire the perfect woman who is totally compliant."

El Sabio: "What a *fercockt* response!"

Ima: "Did anyone try the vibrators that are controlled by phones?"

Ava: "Of course we did. I bought half a dozen for holiday gifts. I'll sell you one."

Jeannette Gedankenlos: "Listen, Dr. Freud; I went to a lecture on ethics where the speaker pointed out that maybe sex dolls have the right to 'Just Say No' to certain unusual requests. Maybe we should consider the robots' wishes. This isn't the Victorian era anymore."

Filbert: "I beg your pardon, Dr. Jeannette. Does that mean I can't bugger my new babe?"

Jeannette: "I think you are a certified degenerate. How did such a low life as you even get into this village?

Filbert: "I'm a Road Scholar!"

Heckler: "Oh, that's why you can't get your mind out of the gutter!"

Jeannette: "Filbert, I hope you'll at least use lubricant if you must engage in such perversions."

Filbert: "What would you recommend, doc?"

Jeannette: "WD-40 or silicone spray."

Filbert: "Thanks; good old WD-40 would have been my first choice. And I've got plenty of it in my garage."

Cara: "She's making fun of you, Fil. Try Astro-glide. Just ask my husband Karl."

Filbert: "So, Doc, when do you think marriage to sex robots will be legal?"

Cara: (interrupts) "What about the male sex robots? It shouldn't always be about you guys getting your jollies."

Karl Chasid: "Honey, you're embarrassing me. Don't I fulfill your every desire?"

Cara: "Sure honey. But when you fall asleep after we do it, I'm still ready to roar. I could go a few more rounds."

Ben: "Cara, I checked into that for you. Male sex robots are currently under development. But the scientists are having trouble getting the metallic men to stay hard."

Bella: (muttering under her breath): "Story of my life."

Buford: "In Asia, affluent families buy their sons sex robots so they don't waste time on relationships and can concentrate on their studies. Now that's another solid market where we could invest."

Jeannette: "I can't believe that's already happening in the Orient. Those people are supposed to be smarter than us because they eat a lot of fish."

Ned: "Nowadays, the politically correct term is Asia. You should know better, Jeannette."

Jeannette: "OK, Filbert. I didn't answer your earlier question. At one of the other workshops that I attended we discussed the ethics of marrying a robot. Someone in the audience speculated on robots marrying each other."

Dr. Freud: "Now, that's a brave new world. Soon we won't need any humans."

El Sabio: "Just you wait. When robots can procreate, you will just have to masturbate."

Jeannette: "There's that voice again. Where is he hiding?"

Filbert: "Please! Enough with the revenge of the academentians! Rather than marry Delilah and reimburse you old coots, I'm going to buy a custom hermaphrodite robot and keep her all to myself."

Delilah: "Easy come, easy go. Filbert. So much for me being your one and only. Where'd that hunky Scott guy go? We could get into all sorts of funky stuff together." Delilah purrs.

Dr. Freud: "Poor Fil. He just doesn't know what he wants. He obviously has a gender bender identity issue. Hmmm. Let me check the DSM to see if that category is still listed."

El Sabio: "What's with all the clinical labels? Filbert is clearly just confused. That DSM is bullshit – whatever version they are up to. Who cares? Filbert just wants the best of both worlds."

Suddenly, El Sabio materializes. He breaks into song and dance:

El Sabio: "You shrinks are stuck in a trance-like state. Us critters don't have time to fritter. When the robots take over, you all will have to bend over and expect a total makeover. When robots breed, expect to bleed."

Heckler: "You're the top dog, El Sabio."

El Sabio: "I'm the big dog."

Heckler: "Not exactly pipsqueak!"

Brunnhilde: (banging her gavel) "Enough already, we still need to hear from the Stoners, I mean the group that represented us at the Cannabis Cup."

Professor Growmore: "Before I make my presentation, I'd like Nancy to talk about a possible new community project. She is our resident Master Gardener. As we become more experienced using the products of our grow, we can update our southwestern cookbook with cannabis recipes. As those of you who were lucky enough to sample the wonderful Moses Magic Matzoh Ball soup at the Engels' community Seder can attest, Nancy has become quite the cannabis cook."

Loud round of applause and whistles

Dr. Freud: "Those were some mighty big balls."

El Sabio: "Is that a Freudian slip?"

Nancy: "I attended a lecture on edibles where someone mentioned their cannabis cookbook. Since we already have one successful community cookbook, we could write our own ganja cookbook. We could call it Marvelous Medicated Meals from the Meadows."

Lillian Lemishkeh: "That's too long for the title, Nancy. You should know better than that."

Nancy: "You're absolutely right, Lillian. How about MmmMmmMmmMmmm with a picture of a huge cannabis leaf? People will get the idea."

Ava: "Meeowww!"

Ned: "That's my Editress X."

Professor Growmore: "Nancy, why don't you tell everyone about the Magical Butter machine you bought after you attended a demonstration?"

Nancy: "Thanks for reminding me Professor Growmore. It's sitting on my kitchen table and I haven't opened the box yet. Everyone ought to have one of these beauties. Perhaps we should think about investing in the company's stocks. The Magical Butter machine will knock Betty Crocker right off her dusty bookshelf.

"For instance, with the machine you can make marijuana-infused cooking oil and medicated butter that you can use in all sorts of edibles from soup and salads to entrees and desserts. Of course, the machine also processes nuggies into tinctures. I'll research to see if they have commercial sizes. That would be a big help in producing our own edibles for the dispensary."

Cara: "Is the oil green?"

Karl: "What a silly question."

Nancy: "Of course it is. Isn't everyone talking about going green? Plus, you can buy green mason jars to add to the aesthetic experience."

Buford: "Let's not forget about the larger consumer base for edibles. At the Cannabis Cup, vendors were giving out medicated doggy treats to bring home to their pets."

Ned: "Now, that's a captive audience. While we were on the plane, Nancy and I were brainstorming about what we'll do after we develop the doggy products. Nancy plans to write a press release to introduce our new line after we figure it out."

Ima: "Slow down a bit. I'm concerned that the extra publicity will bring too many people to Einstein Meadows to buy the medicated doggy treats. Think of the traffic on our dusty desert road crisscrossed with cattle grates!"

The Heckler starts playing "Who Let the Dogs Out" by the Baha Men on his iPhone. Some people start to dance.

Leopold Spieber: "And, we might get a lot of criticism because some people will be afraid that their children could get into the dog treats. We don't want to be hit with a law suit about endangering children."

Dr. Freud: "Their teachers might appreciate a mellowed-out student body."

El Sabio: "That didn't sound right, Dr. Frudito. I'll have to give that some more thought."

The group enthusiastically sings the chorus: "WHO LET THE DOGS OUT? WHO WHO WHO!"

Brunnhilde: (banging the gavel again) "I'm in charge here. And we'll simply set a new rule. You can't bring your dogs into the dispensary under any circumstance."

Ned: (jumps up) "Thank you, Brunnie!" Ned salutes Brunnhilde.

Brunnhilde: "Ned, I know you're allergic to dogs. But you didn't let me finish. We will open a separate dispensary where canines will be welcome."

Ned: "Fine; I misspoke. I take back my compliment. I unsalute you."

Heckler: "That's better than being unfriended."

Dr. Quackenbush: "I commend this proactive measure to protect the health of residents and visitors who are allergic to dogs."

Dr. Freud: "Too bad airlines aren't as considerate."

El Sabio: "Speak for yourself."

Dr. Freud: "The airlines are required to let all *mesheguna* dogs board. That includes you, El Sabio!"

Nancy: "Since it's so important that all dogs have access to medicated treats, we won't discriminate between therapy dogs, companion animals, purebred pets, or just plain mutts. All dogs are welcome in the canine dispensary. Sorry, honey. You and I just won't volunteer in that dispensary."

Ned: "Yes, we have to be politically correct. We don't want any violent protesters storming the neighborhood, setting fires, and looting the dispensary. All Dogs Lives

Matter! Hey, I have a great idea. We should post those signs to protect ourselves: ADLM."

Professor Growmore: "What do you all think about changing the Monged Mongrel line to Cannabis Rx to appeal to a wider audience?"

Dr. Freud: "Well, I like the name Monged Mongrel; it's sexy. But I do think we need to rename some of our marijuana products. You know there are lots of places in the world where people are prejudiced. If we want to do business with these ignoramuses, we could just substitute names for some of our existing products."

El Sabio: "You go Dr. Frudito. What do you think about 'Get Way More Head than the Rest' for our new slogan?"

Buford: "The name Einstein just won't sell in some parts of the world. It's all about marketing. And now we're moving onto the worldwide stage."

Ned: "Yes, in my private conversations at coffeeshops, some international travelers talked about the fact that we might need to rename some of our marijuana products to appeal to a broader, wider, woke audience. Albert Einstein's Going Nuclear can become Getting Bombed. Other ethnically sensitive names could be Knock Knock on the Roof, Baked Bazaar, Open Sesame, Magic Carpet Ride, or Shepherd's Delight."

Professor Growmore: "We still have some more research to do, fellow scientists. At the Cannabis Cup, I scored some magic growing tablets."

Lilith: "What's magic about them? What were they called?"

Professor Growmore: "Jack and the Bean Stalk."

Bella: "That sounds like a mighty big pole. I'd like to climb that trunk."

Professor Growmore: "You are so right Bella. Did you know that marijuana is a great aphrodisiac?"

Heckler: "Can I have an Amen?"

Audience: (emphatically) "AMEN!"

Buford: "I have a super marketing idea. We can place our dispensary business cards in little plastic packets along with three nuggies and drop them from a drone over the nearest city. We can spare 3,000 nuggies; we have millions of them."

Leopold: What a great way to get 1,000 new customers. We will all become billionaires."

Filbert: "Not so fast! You obviously don't read the *Times of Israel*. Two Israelis in Tel Aviv were arrested for a dooby drone drop. People ran into traffic to scoop up those bad boys; some of them landed in schoolyards. You can watch the You Tube video at https://www.youtube.com/watch?V=6iscHOH9yz0."

Buford: "You aren't even Jewish, Fil. What are you doing reading the *Times of Israel*?"

Filbert: "I'm an evangelical Christian and I take a strong interest in our Hebrew friends in Israel."

Rabbi Kaplan: "*Mazel tov* Filbert!"

Dr. Freud: "I second that emotion and I will revise my analysis of you, Filbert. Maybe you shouldn't be classified. I didn't know you were such a humanitarian."

Filbert: "Just because I look like a redneck and don't have a bullshit degree doesn't mean I'm not intelligent and compassionate. After all I strongly believe in Make America Great Again. I proudly wear my red MAGA hat. I always vote twice and I'm a Road Scholar."

Heckler: "You go Filbert!"

El Sabio: "That's Dr. Frudito, always putting a label on behavior. Toss out that *fercockt* DSM V. Those pages aren't fit to tear out and wipe my backside.

Dr. Freud: (sounding like he is making a great pronouncement) "Now, we have to remember it is progress not perfection that should be our guiding belief. We don't need a lot *gelt*; we have too much already."

A loud voice calls from outside the room:

"Excuse me. Excuse me. I have several large boxes out here and I need some assistance getting them off the truck. Maybe some of you youngsters can help me out."

Filbert: "Sure, we can be of service. Whaddya' got there?"

UPS Driver: "I don't know. They're long boxes labeled XXX. They're marked Fragile and I smell perfume coming from them."

Brunnhilde: "Let's take a 15-minute break while the truck is unloaded. Then we'll check out what arrived."

The group leaves for a marijuana-infused tea break.

Brunnhilde: (taps her gavel, grimaces and holds her head): "OK, let's get started. Let's see who these packages are addressed to. Oh, they're from Amsterdam and they're for Buford."

Buford: "They must be the other sex robots we ordered."

Filbert starts to rip open one of the boxes.

Jeannette: "Gently, gently. That's precious cargo there, Fil."

She teases the first box open, but the bottom falls out where Filbert manhandled it. Clouds of scented pink tissue paper and hot pink packing peanuts waft out of the crate.

After Jeannette lifted one of the sex robots out of the crate, it became painfully obvious that some Transit Authority official had had his way with her. Someone had to clean out the violated robot.

Dr. Coconut: "I told you so."

Leopold: "I'd still like to try her out – even if she isn't a virgin. It's hard to find a real virgin these days anyway. Who knows? This one could turn out to be my perfect soul mate. If she can ring my chimes, I'd like to marry her. I'm tired of being alone. Barry can't make me feel like a real man. Filbert shouldn't have all the fun!"

Buford: "Whatever floats your boat, Leo. But, remember, you'll have to reimburse the Meadows for this robot. They were never meant for exclusive use."

Brunnhilde: "Buford is right. The robots are community property for us to research investment opportunities."

Heckler: "What's going on here? Is this a return to the 60's or are we in the love slave trade?"

Leopold: "Brunnhilde, if it turns out that she's the one, would you marry me and my sweetie?"

Brunnhilde: "That's pretty weird, Leopold, and it's not legal yet."

Ava: "Says you, honey."

Dr. Freud (whispering): "You know, helping Leopold and Filbert tie the knot with their robots would be a *mitzvah*."

Brunnhilde: "What the heck is that?"

Dr. Freud: "A *mitzvah* is a commandment from God to do something good every day."

Brunnhilde: "That's not part of my religion."

Dr. Freud: "*Nu*? I'm surprised, that you as an educated woman and a member of the New Age clergy haven't read both versions – the Old and the New. Nevertheless, it will be good for your soul to help Filbert and Leopold with their love lives."

Buford: "Brunnhilde, you know we made a lot of money when you started performing transsexual weddings. This could be a new gold mine for us."

El Sabio: "I always knew humans were going to pot. This confirms it!"

Pink packing peanuts fly all over as Brunnhilde pleads for order.

Brunnhilde: "I recommend you all go take a cold shower. It's getting way too steamy in here. And what's with the air conditioning? I thought we fixed that! Remember, progress not perfection. We'll reconvene another time. This meeting is adjourned."

El Sabio pants. Dr. Freud wipes his spectacles.

Dear Reader, Get ready: Judge Solomon is coming back to the Meadows to deliver more frontier justice. Who will be committed this time? Any guesses?

CHAPTER 9 -

"The Young Man Knows the Rules, But the Old Man Knows the Exceptions"

- Oliver Wendell Holmes, Sr.

If you are one of our senior readers, perhaps you have realized that wisdom is not seeing everything as black or white. Now, if you are one of our younger readers, we don't cotton to having any protesters or rioters on our streets. That's why we live in a Second Amendment open-carry county in a right-to-bear arms state.

So, here's a word of unasked for advice for our younger audience: sometimes it's best to keep our opinions to ourselves. However, since we are both seniors, we are exempt from that advice.

Dr. Freud: (with a very authoritative tone) "Living in a community with a homeowners association isn't always a bowl of cherries. There's a price to be paid for having beautiful grounds and consistency in architecture."

El Sabio: (interrupting) "It's called conformity! Personally, I think people are *mesheguna* to live in such a *fercockt* community. Most HOAs have a long list of rules and a menu of financial penalties. What officious HOA board members don't seem to realize is that solutions don't come if you are just looking at problems."

Ned: "That's why Dr. Freud and I call the academentians mental masturbators of the universe. Of course, one would think that living here at Einstein Meadows, we would have long since escaped such idiocy having become both stoned and naked. But that isn't always the case. Plus, we have way higher IQs than the rest of the general population. What I learned as a psychologist is if you want to step out of the puzzling box, you need to change how you view it or do it."

Nancy: "In this chapter, Judge Solomon returns for another round of open-air court at the Meadows. Each of these five cases will clearly illustrate Oliver Wendell Holmes' famous quotation: 'The young man knows the rules, but the old man knows the exceptions.' As you may remember from an earlier chapter, Judge Solomon, a descendent of the famous hanging Judge Roy Bean, is well-known for his wise but somewhat out-of-the-box verdicts."

Ned: "Some will criticize him for practicing blind justice; we prefer to see him as an old-west male version of Lady Justice. Although there are some nasty rumors circulating about how he lost his vision – including peeking through the wrong hole at the wrong time – we do not engage in such speculation and idle gossip. We leave that to the merry Twitter or Facebook mavens."

El Sabio: "The one thing all of these cases have in common is that even the most enlightened boards can be stuck enforcing ridiculous rules with asinine fines. When all else fails, Judge Solomon prevails! I have no doubt he will sort you out. He loves sending miscreants to the funny farm for an attitude adjustment. In fact, he is even thinking of building a satellite clinic here at the Meadows. Just ask Ned who offered to provide investment capital. He is hoping to involuntarily enroll some HOA board members."

Dr. Freud: "I agree with Ned. That's just what this place needs. As I like to say 'urine analysis' – oh, I think I just misspoke!"

El Sabio: "No problem. The idiots in Congress misspeak all the time. They've made it an art form."

Shoulder Rotator Cuff Tsuris:

Ned: "Our neighbor Karl, a 90-year-old retired judge, who everyone affectionately called Pops, is wobbly on his feet and has a torn rotator cuff. Since we don't have curbside garbage pickup and we must bring trash across the street to a dumpster, getting rid of the trash was very difficult for Pops. He had something large delivered and wanted to get rid of the cardboard box. Because it was impossible for him to reach up and toss the box in the dumpster, Pops left it neatly outside the dumpster. I wished he had asked me for some assistance.

"After an obnoxious neighbor ratted him out, the HOA board levied a $100 fine. The offending box had a label with Pops' address. (Reminds me of Arlo Guthrie getting busted after the cops found a letter with his address on it underneath a mountain of trash on Thanksgiving Day. And we all know how that turned out.)

"Pops objected to the fine and appealed his case to the town court. It was humiliating enough for Pops to rely on a cane, but being fined by the HOA really tested his patience. He acknowledged to me that it would have been easier for him to leave the box on his lawn. But he made the effort to drag it into the dumpster enclosure."

El Sabio: "Sounds like the perfect case for Judge Solomon. Let's wait and see what the bagging Judge decides. In the meantime, I'll get some rope made of hemp to take care of that bitchy neighbor." El Sabio starts to sing quietly, "You can get anything you want at Alice's restaurant, excepting Alice...!")

The open- air court session commences:

Bailiff: "All rise for the honorable Judge Solomon!"

The judge walks in escorted by his seeing eye dog.

Judge Solomon: "OK. I hear you wing nuts are stirring the pot again. And I don't mean the type you all smoke. So, I understand I have five cases to hear today. I have read the briefs and I must say you aren't using enough weed to have so much *tsuris* for such a small neighborhood. I wish I hadn't lost my sight because I would love to see what you look like – especially since you are naked. Karl Chasid, please approach the bench. Have a seat next to me. I've read your complaint. You are obviously innocent and I order the HOA to give you back the $100 fine. Plus, they must give you an additional $100 for wasting your time and mine."

Karl: "Thank you judge."

Judge Solomon: "I would like the informant to approach the bench. Please come a little closer my dear; I want to smell your breath. Whoa! Just as I thought – you smell like a brewery. I sentence you to one month at Briarwood. Do you have anything to say for yourself?"

The ratty neighbor turns around and moons him. Everyone starts laughing.

Judge Solomon: "What just happened here?"

Bailiff: "The bitch mooned you!"

Judge Solomon: "Handcuff her and let Rusty take a bite out of her ass. Next case."

The Three-Flag Dilemma:

Ned, Nancy, Reverend Verschwender, and Brother Gunther strategize before Judge Solomon hears this case.

Ned: "In Einstein Meadows, only three flags are allowed: a Cannabis flag, the American flag of course, and the Confederate flag. Lest some of you politically liberal readers (if we have any) be offended, keep in mind that Einstein Meadows is in a state that was once a great Confederate territory."

Reverend Vernon Verschwender: "That's right Brother Ned. Here in the southwest, the Civil War is often referred to as the 'war of northern aggression.' Yankee transplants – including you former New Yorkers – call it the 'war between the states.' In the South, we recognize and embrace our history and do not allow outsiders to cancel our culture or remove our statues."

Nancy: (speaking directly to the Reverend) "The new arrivals from the East who moved in next door to you objected to the large Confederate flag flying atop a 30-foot flag pole. The newer newbies also took exception to Brother Gunther's equally large Confederate flag that they could see across the wash. They had purchased their house sight unseen."

Brother Gunther Shaygetz: "I won't take it down because I want Sister Misty to see it as a landmark so she can find her way home."

Reverend Vernon: "Well bless those Yankees' hearts; this flag has been in my family since the Battle of Gettysburg. It will fly as long as I am alive and beyond!"

The Heckler starts playing "Dixie" on his iPhone. Almost the entire audience spontaneously stands. They take off their hats and hold them over their hearts and start singing, "I wish I was in the land of cotton. Old times there are not forgotten. Look away! Look away! Look away Dixieland."

Judge Solomon: "I would like Reverend Verschwender to approach the bench. Reverend, your great grandpappy and mine served together at the famous battle in Pennsylvania. They gave those Yanks a run for their money. Many good people died on our side. There is nothing wrong with Confederate flags – every true American of southern descent has one. You Yankees should get a life. If you want to live in the south, you should respect our customs – or move back to your crime ridden Democratically controlled cities. Will the person who made this complaint please approach the bench?"

Bailiff: "Do you swear to tell the whole truth even though you are a Northerner?"

Yankee complainer: "I don't think it is fair to allow my neighbors to fly the Confederate flag."

Judge Solomon: "You are entitled to your opinion but you Demonrats are wrong! If I hear of this matter again, I'll send you to Briarwood for an indefinite stay. You can join the other patients with TDS. Next case!"

El Sabio: "I like this judge's no-nonsense approach. I wonder if he sells shares for Briarwood. It sounds like a money-making machine."

Heckler: "At least he is not hanging them."

The Troublesome Outhouses:

Siegfried Zynismus: (in an annoyed tone) "Our three new outhouses are missing the traditional half-moon. The Campus Oversight Committee followed Chief El Guappo's suggestions and placed them on a walking trail more than a mile from the nearest water pipe, where it would have been cost prohibitive to put in plumbing. So, the environmentally sensitive and politically correct members of the GPsC (green privy sub-committee) installed composting toilets."

Heckler: "Are they vegans? And, why are there three bathrooms instead of two?"

Ned: "One says Boys, one says other Girls, and the third Confused."

Dr. Freud: "That's ridiculous! They can just pull their waistband and see what equipment they have. It's either one or the other."

Ned: "I think people could just pee in the desert – but they are too embarrassed by the potential lack of privacy and concerned about prickly bushes. Frenchie wanted to erect a pissoir like they have on Paris streets, but the Einstonians thought that would be too gross. But it would be private."

Chief El Guappo: "Listen my white friends. Our Apache tribe donated these handcrafted outhouses and placed them near a beautiful vista overlooking the canyon and surrounding mountains."

Ned: "OK, the outdoor facilities and the land they sat on were donated. However, since the GPC members forgot to ask the Board of Health for approval, the town officials ordered that the outhouses remain locked pending BOH review and approval. The HOA and GPC didn't have a problem with the facilities being locked."

Chief El Guappo: "Where's my tomahawk? I still can lead my people into battle whenever I think it is necessary. We're getting rusty with scalping. I objected and filed a complaint with the court."

Judge Solomon: "Now this sounds like an interesting dilemma. The outhouse sits on ancient tribal land. But it appears there is a conflict of interest here. Will Chief El Guappo approach the bench? Shalom Chief!"

Bailiff: "Do you swear to tell the truth?"

Chief El Guappo: "Of course, only white men swear with crooked tongue."

The chief turns to the assembled crowd and sticks out his tongue.

Heckler: "That Indian's tongue is as straight as an arrow!"

Everyone laughs.

Judge Solomon: "What did I miss?"

Bailiff: "He just stuck his tongue out to the audience."

Judge Solomon: "Good for you."

Chief El Guappo: "People need to have reasonable access to bathroom facilities according to federal law. So, the authorities are wrong. The only thing we did wrong is forget to put a half-moon on the door. But we have punished the carpenter by branding his butt with the Bar E Triple I ranch iron."

Judge Solomon: "Now that's a fitting punishment for your carpenter. Without half-moons on the doors, those outhouses are obviously not kosher."

Chief El Guappo: "We even built a third outhouse to humor the socially conscious idiots on the town council. It seems only you white folks don't know whether you are a boy or girl. We think that's bizarre."

Judge Solomon: "I agree with your gender comments Chief. Too bad we must live with ding-a-ling pronouncements of senior Washington leaders. But you have your own sovereign nation so you can do what you want."

Chief El Guappo: "Thank you your honor, you have renewed my faith in the system. I figured anyone who is a decendent of the famous hanging Judge Bean must be an upstanding jurist. But I still won't pay any federal taxes."

Judge Solomon: "Let's get to the heart of the matter. Chief, you are right. This outhouse sits on Apache land that was stolen by my ancestors. You can remove the lock. The town Board of Health has no jurisdiction from my point of view. You don't have to wait for those obnoxious town bureaucrats to make up their minds. They are worse than the officious yo-yos who run this place."

Heckler: "Let me hear an Amen!"

The crowd responds with a loud Amen.

Judge Solomon: "Chief, if the town sends any officials here, don't let them in. Scalp them if you want, or call the Sheriff. We will have them arrested and sent to Briarwood. On second thought, I think we will give them lobotomies so you don't have to scalp them. That will mellow them out. Maybe it will cure their TDS. Next case!"

Your Car is Too Old

Ned: (having a quiet conversation with Nancy)

"This is personal because it concerns our beloved 2008 Jeep Wrangler X. There is no more iconic American car than the Jeep except perhaps the Model T. The Jeep defines the American West."

Nancy: "You're so right, sweety. Some snooty HOA board members didn't like the fact that we had an unwashed 12-year-old car in the parking lot of the community center.

"The powers-that-be were concerned about the optics of everyone driving into Einstein Meadows passing by our classic Jeep. And, they issued a $100 fine each day until we moved the car. Don't forget that two of our neighbors hogged the guest spots and the off-street parking was eliminated."

Ned: "Even before Einstein Meadows hosted so many newly minted millionaires, the streets were already lined with the usual Mercedes, Audis, Lexus, BMWs, Aston Martins, Cadillacs, Jaguars, and a few Bentleys. In fact, we keep our Audi TT roadster in the garage. No sense in letting pack rats chew the wires. You just don't mess with a man's Jeep. Everyone knows that. So, that's why I brought it before Judge Solomon."

The Bailiff announces the next case.

Dr. Ray Rising Sun: (acting as Ned's advocate) "The Einstonians particularly don't like the nasty American eagles on the doors and the fact that the Engels advertise their first novel on the rear tire cover of the Jeep. The crazed HOA board wanted them to pay for advertising space. Nancy threatened to shove the $100 bill up their butts or down their throats – whatever they preferred."

Judge Solomon: "I admire your spunk, Nancy. Ned, you must be very proud of your wife. I miss being able to drive my own Jeep. Perhaps you noticed that the bailiff drove me here in my bright red Jeep. You know 'ticket me red'. Except no cop in this county has the balls to ticket the bailiff because he will shoot their nuts off. Ned, I rule that you don't have to pay these officious board members the $100. But you will have to take the doors off."

Nancy: "But Judge!"

Judge Solomon: "That's the verdict."

Dr. Freud: "Now that's a case of lopsided blind justice."

Shared Driveway Dispute

A separate issue was when we had to park our Jeep in the shared driveway after Nancy had a ski incident that made it impossible for her to walk down to the community center parking lot where we usually parked. We only parked there long enough for Nancy to hobble out and get into the house. And Nancy was working hard to pick up her pace.

Judge Solomon: "Now on to the second complainant, Lillian Lemishkeh, please approach the bench."

Lillian: "Can my horse Trombenik accompany me?"

Judge Solomon: "Absolutely not! This is already a freak show. I've heard you like to talk to your horse and he talks to you. You are obviously several sandwiches short of a picnic. I sentence you to three months at Briarwood for being such an inconsiderate neighbor. However, since I am fair minded, you can take your horse with you. We'll put you both up in the stable."

The bailiff drags Lillian out of the court room screaming.

Judge Solomon: "OK I've heard enough *bupkes* for a week. This community has too many ridiculous rules. You need to work on minimizing your regulations. As the famous jurist Oliver Wendell Homes, Sr. once said, 'the young man knows the rules, but the old man knows the exceptions.' Court adjourned!"

Dear Reader,

If you are one of our mature readers, we hope you still take time each day to play – not just look at your stock portfolio or watch cable news. If you aren't setting aside enough time for fun and just plain silliness, this next chapter is very important.

CHAPTER 10 -

We Don't Stop Playing Because We Grow Old. We Grow Old Because We Stop Playing

– George Bernard Shaw

Dr. Freud and Ned sit outside under the ramada.

Dr. Freud: "So, Ned how do you explain that you look much younger than your physical age?"

El Sabio materializes and attempts to hijack the conversation.

El Sabio: "I'll answer that for him."

Ned: "Excuse me but I was the one who was asked the question. I'm not like the recent presidential candidate who ducked questions by hiding in his basement. I still have all my faculties! Dr. Freud, I have always believed that the secret to youthfulness as a senior is never losing your inner child."

El Sabio: "I think you meant outward child!"

Ned: "Look, we all know people who were 40 when they were 20 and I'm not talking about having an old soul. In my practice as a psychologist, kids frequently asked me – 'What's it like to be an adult?' I would reply – Go ask your parents – I'm just a grownup kid."

Dr. Freud: "So what did the parents say?"

Ned: "Go ask the kids. I'm not the one in analysis!"

El Sabio: "Yeah Frudito – analyze that!"

Dr. Freud: "Well El Sabio, you probably don't have all the chairs under the table. I hear what you are saying Ned. We have less energy as we age. But if we exercise, watch what we eat, try to learn new things, have plenty of weed, wear a *tallit and tzitzis,* black socks and a bow tie, we certainly can improve our outlook."

El Sabio: "Did you know that marijuana is a great aphrodisiac?"

Dr. Freud: "What does that have to do with anything?"

El Sabio: "You're slipping Frudito! Don't you remember your early theories? Libido is crucial and if you don't act on your id, your weenie will shrink. Just ask Filbert der Dorftrottel. Yo Bert, come over here, por favor."

Filbert is walking by the ramada and suddenly stops.

Filbert: "What's up you little *pisher*?"

El Sabio: "I just shared your pecker is too small for bar room betting."

Filbert: "Bullshit!" (He drops his pants.)

El Sabio: "¡Ai caramba! Lo siento! Does anyone have a yardstick? That's more than 30 centimeters – let's go to the nearest bar and make a killing."

Filbert: "I know I have opinion on everything. That's why I am nicknamed Filbert on the mount. I wear that title proudly. If I only had a dollar for each of my pearls of wisdom, I would be a billionaire instead of a common millionaire.

Dr. Freud: "You are both *fercockt!*"

If you neglect yourself, you'll spoil

Ned: "Let's get back to the original topic. It's very hard to follow the conversation when you guys interrupt each other and me. I think it is important to treat every day as if it's your birthday."

Dr. Freud: "Yes, make it a point to shine and be your best self."

Ned: "It's also vital to share your special gifts with people."

Filbert: "Yeah my one-eyed monster is always looking for new watering holes."

Ned: "I'm not talking about that, you degenerate. I mean sharing your expertise like teaching fellow seniors auto mechanics, water aerobics, tai chi, jewelry making, etc. To stay youthful, expand your hobbies and share positive energy."

Nancy: (who has been sitting quietly by Ned's side) "And speaking of positive energy, we could host workshops on Tantric love."

Filbert: "Well I could teach them about varmint control and skillful voyeurism."

Dr. Freud: "Why don't you tell them how you got busted looking up women's dresses while they rode the escalators in New York?"

Filbert: "It was only a misdemeanor with a $20 fine. I had forgotten about that. I miss Manhattan. As you know, here in this small Western city there aren't too many opportunities for that delightful pastime since most buildings are only one story."

Dr. Freud: "Ned and Nancy are onto something. Everyone here participates in senior Olympics even if they're not Charles Atlas. It's important to have athletic challenges, show up for classes, and keep trying to better yourself."

Ned: "Where did El Sabio go? He seems to have just disappeared. He might like the idea of Tantric love with your soulmate workshops."

Filbert: "I'm sure he would. But we will have to broaden the title to expand the potential audience. Not everyone is as lucky as you and Nancy. After all I only have a sex robot for companionship."

El Sabio: (suddenly reappears) "Did I hear my name mentioned?"

Filbert: "You always show up out of nowhere. We were talking about Tantric love."

El Sabio: "You sure are a bunch of horny old codgers. Now I know why you like the Hooters for Cooters restaurant in the neighboring community. Of course, you can experience a higher state of consciousness. I suggest you visit the Tantric temple in the nearby city, if it is still in business. The last I heard those conservative freaks in our state's government didn't like people having free love. They mistook people giving donations as paying for prostitution. Maybe that has changed since so many people have fled those Demonrat states of California and Washington."

Leopold and Ava stop to join the conversation.

Leopold Spieber: "Yeah, but they bring their old voting habits with them. You know only half the population has intelligence. Plus, many people vote against their own self-interest because of stupid party loyalty."

El Sabio: "Yes, that is true. Leopold, if you enroll in a workshop you can get some new ideas and expertise. You will just have to leave your six guns at home. I know the Tantric temple number by heart. Give them a ring and say Dr. Love Doggie sent you."

Filbert: "Do you think I could bring Scarlett?"

Dr. Freud: "Probably not; but give it a shot!"

El Sabio: "Filbert I recommend Golden Retriever position for you."

Filbert: "If you mean doggy-style, I'm your man. Scarlett loves to moan."

Dr. Freud: "Ah hah! Now I know why you wanted a hermaphrodite sex robot."

No matter how you feel, get up, dress up and show up

Ned: "If people aren't having a good day, they just need to try to get started. You know our Ask the Seniors column for the region has brought us a lot of recognition. Plus, we have kept up our university required mission of community outreach even though we are now retired. Public service is important."

Filbert: "Speak for yourself. I'm not a retired academentian. I charge for my expertise. Especially since I don't have a bullshit degree."

Leopold: "I still carry my business card. Do you want one?"

Ned: "What am I supposed to do with it?"

Leopold: "Don't ask me. I just have them. Oh, now I remember. I give them out in the Ponderosa room when we meet potential new residents. I like to present them with my credentials."

El Sabio: "That's absurd – everyone in this neighborhood has an advanced degree. It's either a Piled High in Dung (Ph.D.), Mad Dog (MD), Just Dingbat (JD), one Psychologically Disturbed (Psy.D.), and an Eat Donkey Doo (Ed.D.). So, what's the big deal?"

Ava Sinnlich: "You're just so cute little poochie." (rubbing his belly and touching his ears)

Leopold: "El Sabio, Keep your opinions to yourself, you little mutt! You are no posh toddy."

El Sabio: "That comment doesn't deserve a verbal response." (He passes gas loudly.) "Take that you opinionated dog-hating wind bag!"

Leopold: "Let's hold a gala to celebrate the fifth-year anniversary of the Great Einstein Meadows Ganja Experiment. We can get a lot of people together in one place and get them out of their haciendas."

Time to Reminisce

So, we prepared for a day-long celebration. Some Meadowites break off into smaller groups to reminisce. Most of the Einstonians want to party, but others like Ned, Dr. Freud, and Leopold commemorate the milestone by

167

reflecting on the journey. They want to recall events that demonstrated growth. Then they'll party.

Ned plays one of his favorite Woodstock tunes on his iPhone, "A Long Time Coming" by Crosby, Stills, Nash and Young.

Dr. Freud: "The Einstein Meets Esalen Institute has been a great success. The biggest accomplishment to date was holding a community wide meditation day. You guys have become very altruistic."

Ava: "Don't forget our inspired community painting project of the Woodstock bus."

Scott Gonzaga: "That worked out great, if I do say so myself. The bus is still helping us spread the word about the good life here at the Meadows when we drive it around town to events."

Leopold: "And our sex dungeon is no longer hidden."

El Sabio: "We have an amazing openness to robotic sex dolls. Now several dolls are cohabitating with the senior neighbors."

Dr. Quackenbush: "That will cut down on all the sexually transmitted diseases so prevalent in some adult neighborhoods."

Dr. Freud: "Of course. But Filbert is a new man. And the Einstonians seem to recognize that no matter how you feel, you can get up, dress up and show up. They have realized: if you neglect yourself, you'll spoil."

Filbert: "Thanks, Dr. Freud. I'm glad you noticed the difference. I feel so gratified that Brunnhilde married Scarlett and me, my robotic hermaphrodite. She looks like a high-maintenance babe. But she is almost zero upkeep. It's too bad my buddies from the old neighborhood can't make that claim. I don't have to pay for food, dining out or buy many clothes since we are naked here. Nor does Scarlett need makeup – just lots of silicone spray."

Ned: "We even have ganga growing workshops available to adults in the entire region."

El Sabio: "Now that's very community minded."

Leopold: "Speak for yourself, we are losing money."

Sister Misty returns – rebirth and renewal?

If you read our first novel, you probably remember the contentious debate about marijuana growing and laugh about it. Sister Misty Pashkudnik was the most vociferous opponent to Ned and Nancy's medical marijuana proposal – damning the Einstonians for even considering medicinal marijuana. And if that wasn't enough, she attempted to burn down our first grow.

Now that we are experts at growing and dispensing, it seemed appropriate for Sister Misty to make a surprise appearance. Misty was never too far away. If you recall, she escaped from the police car while the officers were having donuts and fled into the mountains. She didn't want to be committed to the funny farm (Briarwood) and thought she could survive in the federal forest.

Unbeknownst to the Meadowites, she was secretly texting Brother Gunther Shaygetz when she was at a low-enough elevation to get a cell signal. She told Brother Gunther that after she escaped from the Froussards' squad car, she scurried up Apple Mountain which rose 10,000 feet above Einstein Meadows. Ever the resourceful one, Misty snatched clothes off people's lines to keep warm and grabbed a sheet to wrap the clothes in. She knew it got cold on the mountain. Not knowing how long she would be on her own in the federal forest, Misty also raided vegetables from people's gardens and stuffed everything into her homemade bed-sheet rucksack. Luckily for Misty, she grew up in a survivalist family and knew how to live off the land.

As it turned out, the forest had plenty of nuts and berries for her to forage, plus fresh water. So, she was all set. She wandered 40 days and 40 nights on her own before she stumbled on a guerilla ganja grow encampment deep in the forest.

The ganga farmers embraced Misty and gave her food and shelter in exchange for working on the grow. The farmers realized that even their ultra-mellow flock could use some tending and asked Misty, as a former nun, to minister to their spiritual needs. The guerilla farmers grew even more fond of Misty after they learned she had escaped from the law despite being hogtied. Misty explained that she was able to get out of the ropes because she was triple jointed.

Sister Misty texted some vague details about the hidden grow to Brother Gunther when she first came upon the compound. However, since the farmers made her promise to keep their operation confidential and off the fed's radar, she withheld most details until she could speak to Brother Gunther in person. But even then, she swore Brother Gunther to secrecy and carefully scanned the area for listening devices. After all she is still a wanted fugitive.

Brother Gunther later related Misty's strange tale to Ned after Misty returned to Einstein Meadows. Here's how Brother Gunther recalled the conversation.

Sister Misty Pashkudnik: "Gunther, you would have been so proud of me. I spread the Word to a wild assortment of hippies, former motorcycle gang members, army deserters and illegals. My Sunday sermons were always popular."

Brother Gunther: "Could the popularity of your sermons have anything to do with the fact that your congregants were always baked?"

Sister Misty: "I guess that's possible. But I prefer to think I was enlightened and preached with a new found passion."

The guerilla growers assigned Misty the job of bud trimming. Turns out she had a real knack for it. She approached it on a spiritual level and was able to coax the maximum THC from each nuggie. An unexpected benefit of working on the buds was that Misty experienced an ongoing contact high.

The weed liberated Misty's long-repressed libido. She relished her new euphoric state so much that she ultimately yielded and got high directly and intentionally.

Brother Gunther was excited about the anniversary party and wished Misty could join the party. Lo and behold, she did return. But not before she promised the guerilla growers that she would be back within a fortnight to help trim the buds, continue to minister to the growers, and serve as their Tantric love goddess since she now believed in free love and had a wild libido.

When Misty retuned to Einstein Meadows, she asked to address the entire community. Remember, in our first novel, Misty always wore a nun's habit? Now, she was totally naked except for her nun's veil. The

Einstonians were amazed to see so many nasty tattoos and piercings – gifts from her new friends, the ganga farmers. And peeking out from under her veil, her previously jet-black hair had turned snow white.

> *Dear Reader,*
> *Do you remember the roof-raising, barn-storming, soul-scorching Biblical smackdown that Misty pummeled the Einstonians with when we proposed medical marijuana in our first novel? If Misty says she now has even more passion preaching to the weed farmers, then we can only conclude that we have seriously underestimated the mighty power of the sacred plant. No wonder her hair turned white.*

Sister Misty: "I ask for your forgiveness. I recognize that I was too opinionated and judgmental. I deeply apologize for attempting to burn down the grow. I have seen the light and realize that ganga is the Lord's gift to the world. Speaking of seeing the light, let me just whip it out."

Everyone gasped when Misty pulled out her vintage 'flick my dick' penis-shaped cigarette lighter.

As Sister Misty waved around the ignited lighter, people nearly *plotzed* and collectively lost their *kishkas*. Filbert grabbed a fire extinguisher and ran toward the podium.

Sister Misty: "Relax folks. Sheesh, one arson attempt and everyone panics."

Misty then takes out a pocket-sized peace pipe filled with 'Albert Einstein's Going Nuclear' and lights it. She inhales deeply.

The audience sighs in relief.

Sister Misty: "Ahh, that's more like it. The Afghan blends my ganja farmers use helped me to find my inner child. It had been lost! I now treat every day like it's my birthday – maybe you already know that. By the way weed is a great aphrodisiac! But your old tried and true 'Albert Einstein's Going Nuclear' mellows me out and binds me irrevocably to you my brothers and sisters here at the Meadows. I hope you don't mind if I bring back a batch of seeds to share with my new friends in the forest. Speaking of my inner child, we are all living proof that 'we don't stop playing because we grow old. We grow old because we stop playing,' as George Bernard Shaw once said."

Ava: "Amen to that!"

Everyone claps! Misty receives a standing ovation.

> *Dear reader, Wow! We are nearing the end of this sequel. You are about to receive a very important lesson. Do you feel enlightened yet?*

CHAPTER 11 –

Everyone Must Own Up to the

Consequences of Their Actions

Have you ever wanted to get even, prayed for divine retribution, or hatched a plan for justice? Of course. We all have. But, have you thought about the potential consequences?

Those of you who read our first novel probably remember that we introduced a new neighbor in the last chapter. Ms. Lilith entered Einstein Meadows just before the now infamous bon voyage block party. If you've read the Old Testament, you may have encountered this ageless creature. It is not a coincidence that she arrived just in time to witness the shotgun eviction of the Dybbuk/Chaleria family.

Nancy and Ned enjoy the shade of a large mesquite tree in the community garden by the stream. After the big anniversary party, they fondly recall the events of the past five years. Brunnhilde walks over and asks if she can join them on the bench.

Brunnhilde Meeskeit: "Hi. I hope you don't mind company. I baked too many magic brownies and wondered if you would like some."

Nancy: "Yummy. Please sit down and join us. Ned and I were just talking about how Morgana told me that she and Ms. Lilith were colleagues at Wormwood Prep."

Brunnhilde: "You don't say. Hmmm, that explains her sudden arrival. One headache leaves as another potential pain in the *tuchis* moves in."

Ned: "Honey, I thought Morgana asked you to keep it a secret."

Nancy: "Technically she did, but since she and her family were evicted and don't live here anymore, I no longer thought it mattered. In retrospect we're lucky that Ms. Lilith fit right into the neighborhood.

"She didn't live up to our preconceived expectations. She actually enjoys our naked freedom and appreciates the therapeutic effect that doggy marijuana has on Wilfred, her pet Pomeranian."

Ned: "Plus she really likes your weekly column on cannabis cooking. Too bad the regional paper couldn't get it syndicated because of the poorly informed and narrow-minded yo-yos in Congress."

Nancy: "Good food is always the way to a woman's heart."

Ned: "That's true! The fact that Ms. Lilith decided not to wreak havoc on the neighborhood truly illustrates the magical, transformative powers of the weed."

Nancy: "Or perhaps the sacred plant gave Ms. Lilith the insight that it's neither productive nor neighborly to seek retribution at others' expense. Who would have thought a demon could be rehabilitated?"

Brunnhilde: "That's an interesting notion! Here, at Einstein Meadows our neighborhood has many happy residents, but our community has become the favorite target of outside agitators. You know – those folks who don't like the idea of people running around naked, enjoying ganga, holding transgender weddings, making millions of dollars selling marijuana, providing pot to dogs, and genuinely endorsing a hedonistic lifestyle."

Nancy: "Yes, we always have plenty of gawkers at our annual garage sale where all the neighborhood volunteers are naked." Nancy takes a bite of brownie.

"But back to Ms. Lilith. We first met her at the bon voyage party for her departing friends the Dybbuks."

Ned: "That sure was one heck of a celebration. Lilith got to see the Einstonians at their best! I can still picture it. I loved that Filbert took out the Bar E Triple I branding iron. That whole event reminds me of an anonymously authored parable about a farmer and a donkey that was placed on my desk at work. At that time, I was a union grievance chair attempting to reconcile disputes without having to go to arbitration. Of course, mediating between two parties who both felt they were right was nearly impossible. There can be no easy compromise when people are stuck in their positions. Just look at Congress.

"Oh, before I forget, Lilith probably realized that everyone must own up to the consequences of their actions, so she made a good choice. Unfortunately, we all know people who need to be reminded that it's not always smart to act on their impulses without considering the potential impact; folks who speak their mind or rush to judge without knowing all the facts. They don't anticipate the possible blowback that will surely come their way."

Dear Reader,

I assume by now you want to know what parable was placed on my desk. Please note, you copyright enforcers (probably the same idiots who like to block Facebook or Twitter accounts – sorry we don't use social media), we would like to give credit where credit is due. But alas, we do not know the original source of this short story since it is probably hundreds if not thousands of years old. We have discovered there are many different versions of it on the Internet; but, none of them named the authors. So, we thank all of you. I hope you are inspired by this fable.

Dr. Freud and El Sabio walk by and stop to join the conversation.

Dr. Freud: "We heard you were about to share the story of the farmer and the donkey."

El Sabio: "Yes, we came here to provide some commentary and show how it relates to officious HOA board members and the mindless denizens who follow them without thinking."

Brunnhilde: "Wait a minute. How could you know what we were talking about?"

Dr. Freud: "Don't you know? We exemplary psychiatrists can read minds."

El Sabio: "Plus we have telepathic powers!"

Dr. Freud: (in an authoritative tone) "Please hand that to me before you read it. I must review this *bubba meise* to see if it's kosher and psychologically sound advice."

El Sabio: "Not so fast, Dr. Frudito. We psychiatrists are not supposed to give advice. We only dispense medication and sage wisdom when we can't help ourselves. Lesser trained mental health practitioners can provide therapy."

Ned: "El Sabio, you are only partially right. Experienced psychologists know that they should assist others to utilize their own resources to come up with their unique solution paths."

OK. Here's the story:

One day a farmer's donkey fell into a well

The animal whimpered piteously for hours as the farmer tried to figure out what to do. Finally, he decided the animal was old, and the well needed to be covered up anyway. And . . . it just wasn't worth it to retrieve the donkey.

He invited all his neighbors to come and help him. They each grabbed a shovel and began to shovel dirt into the well to cover the donkey.

At first, the donkey realized what was happening and moaned horribly. Then, to everyone's amazement, he quieted down. A few shovels-full later, the farmer looked down the well, and was astonished at what he saw.

As every shovel of dirt hit his back, the donkey shook it off and took a step up. As the farmer's neighbors continued to shovel dirt on top of the animal, he continued to shake it off and take another step up. Everyone was amazed when the donkey stepped up and out over the edge of the well and trotted off.

Dr. Freud: "Now, here is my interpretation. I see this as a dream within a dream."

El Sabio: "Listen Dr. Frudito, you are no Carlos Castaneda!"

Dr. Freud: "Woof!" (barks)

Brunnhilde: "Here's the moral:

Life is going to shovel dirt on you, all kinds of dirt. The trick to getting out of your well is to shake off that dirt and take a step up. Each of our troubles is a stepping stone. We can get out of the deepest wells just by not stopping, by never giving up! Shake it off and take a step up!

Remember my five golden rules for happiness:

1. Free your heart from hatred.

2. Free your mind from worries.

3. Live simply. 4. Give more. 5. Expect less."

Dr. Freud: "*Oy*! Enough of that bullshit . . . Tell it the way it really happened!"

Brunnhilde: "Fine! I may have sugar-coated it a bit. But it's so pleasant here by the stream, and everyone is very mellow. You can't blame me for not wanting to be a buzz-kill. The donkey later came back, caught the farmer out in his field and kicked the *kishkas* out of him. Then he went over to each of the neighbors' farms and kicked the *kishkas* out of them too for helping the farmer."

Dr. Freud: "That's closer. But we're all adults here. Now for the real moral: When you try to cover your ass, it ALWAYS comes back to get you!"

El Sabio: "Dr. Frudito, you seem to have forgotten that the Good Book teaches us that it is important to forgive those who have offended us."

Dr. Freud: "That's true. But it doesn't hurt to spank them first!"

So, What's the Point?

Brunnhilde: "Living in a retirement community will always have its perils and thrills. The price for the shared resources of an organized development inevitably requires some potential sacrifice of individual freedom. It's important for your integrity/self-worth to know where to draw the line."

Ned: "I like to think that the person who anonymously left this parable on my office desk was trying to be helpful. Nancy and I believe one needs to know when to accommodate and when to hold your ground."

Brunnhilde: "Contrary to what many board members believe, homeowners association rules are not written in stone. Courts often have a different opinion when it comes to HOA bullying or unfair or discriminatory application of their rules. In the spirit of harmony, we would like you to think about how this may apply to you and your neighbors. Please work out differences in a calm and respectful manner!"

Dr. Freud: "Remember, everyone has to own up to the consequences of their actions. If you act aggressively toward a member of the community without knowing the whole story, and worse yet get others to join in your *mishegoss*, you give true meaning to the word assume ass – u – me. Treat others as you would like them to treat you."

El Sabio: "As the Buddha said, 'Conquer anger with non-anger. Conquer badness with goodness. Conquer meanness with generosity. Conquer dishonesty with truth.' Take that Frudito. I have the last word this time."

Dear Readers:

Thanks for reading our second novel. We appreciate your support. Now that medical marijuana is legal in 36 states, it's time to get "Einstein Meadows" on the big screen as a movie or TV show. We already wrote a screenplay for the pilot episode. We could use an introduction to Hollywood.

Join the Einstein Meadows movement if you know anyone who can help make this dream a reality. Please send an email to us at: createmiracles@einsteinmeadows.com

---

So, what will happen next at Einstein Meadows? That's easy. In his review of our first novel, Dr. Norm, a former colleague, suggested an interesting title possibility: "Einstein Meadows: Out to Pasture." He saw it as the story of two alter kockers crusading to reform their assisted care living residence before they forget for what they are fighting. As luck would have it, Einstein Meadows already has two assisted living buildings. Thanks Dr. Norm.

       This is one possible direction. We really don't know where the Einstonians journey will take them? Do you have any predictions? Email your ideas to us at createmiracles@einsteinmeadows.com.

To be continued . . .

CHAPTER 12 - Residents' Reactions

Some of you may remember that we gave our neighbors at Einstein Meadows free pre-publication copies of our first novel so they had a chance to comment on how they were treated. Of course, we believe we represented everyone fairly. However, not everyone felt that way – tough nuggies – it's fiction so get a life! As my mentors Mark Twain and Alfred E. Neuman said "Good ideas are worth repeating; especially if they are humorous." So, we bravely let our neighbors sound out again.

"It's Dr. El Sabio. I am a distinguished psychiatrist and don't you forget it! Thank you for giving me a chance to comment on your work of art. I guess you didn't know I was around when you wrote your first novel. I can't say I blame you. After all I was invisible just like Dr. Frudito, my arch rival. Living in this village for several years gives true meaning to why humans need three people to change a light bulb. Two to twirl the ladder and one to hold onto the bulb. I wonder if sex robots could do a better job."

– El Sabio, MD

"Just because I am hard of hearing doesn't mean *I don't deserve respect. You have to speak louder." –* Mr. What

"First of all, learn how to spell my last name correctly. It's Meeskeit not Mieskeit. OK; that said; you were kinder to me this time. Thanks for sharing that I evolved as a person. Who else would marry a sex robot and a human being? I was the first!" – Brunnhilde Meeskeit "

Mazel tov! Finally, we have a novel written by white people who respect the Native American contribution to our society. Plus, we are making you all millionaires at Einstein Meadows." – Chief El Guappo

"Living among you academicians is a transformational experience. It seems that once you shed your clothes you rediscovered your id and dropped most of the bullshit. Now I know what Jimmy Hendrix was talking about."

– Dr. Freud

"This novel is excellent! Who says sequels can't be better than the original? I still have my sailing yacht, so I hope to see you naked again in the Grenadines. I'll have my copy ready for you to sign."

– Marguerite Ingenieux (aka topless sailor)

"It's because of you two that we started bickering again."

– Cara and Karl Chasid

"I am going to track down that skeevy bitch for sharing details about my past life as a sailor. I do wish to thank you for continuing to honor Trombenik, my talking horse. It's a good thing too – otherwise he might take a dump on your shoes." – Lillian Lemishkeh

"The Einstonians were huge slobs and cheapskates. It took all morning to clean up the mess they made. Plus, where was my tip? It's a good thing the manager banned them from this hotel. All I have to say to you is gai kaken oifen yam" – The Chambermaid

"Einstein Meadows is surviving and thriving because your ideas and creative spirit saved the neighborhood. I backed the community garden when the HOA foolishly resisted the idea. That was the start of our fabulous green grow."

– Scott Gonzaga

"I am getting tired of being portrayed as a red neck hick because I am a Road Scholar! However, I'm glad you helped me get a new soul mate; even though she is a robot. Scarlett dutifully obeys my every command. She satisfies my desires wherever and whenever I want. I bet no one married to a human can claim that."

– Filbert der Dorftrottel

"You two are so kind to keep my identity a secret. Now, I can't be cancelled. In these trying times I don't want any crazed leftists banging on my front door or spray painting my garage." – Heckler

"Thanks for bringing back my sweetheart Sister Misty. However, I don't appreciate your turning her into a Tantric love babe. I'm not interested in sharing. You guys are still godless heathens." – Brother Gunther Shaygetz

"Thanks for reuniting me with Brother Gunther. I also appreciate you not treating me like a whack-a-doodle even though I am bipolar. I have to admit I knew people would plotz when I whipped out my vintage pink penis cigarette lighter." – Sister Misty Pashkudnik

"Your novel is very fair and balanced, just like the news network I used to watch. Of course, the devil is in the details! I look forward to your next project. A word to the wise: keep me on your good side." – Ms. Lilith

"The Seder was scrumptious. It's great that so many attractive Christians were there. Thanks for bringing our Hebrew traditions to a wider audience. It was the first Seder experience for most of them. Plus, that was the best

Moses matzoh ball soup I've ever had. You obviously added some magical ingredients." – Rabbi Kaplan

"The Seder was a big hit and I enjoyed watching my brother officiate. Thanks for using a shortened Haggadah." – Reverend Vernon Verschwender

"That was the most amazing Seder I have ever been to. It was the first one I attended naked. The medicated matzoh ball soup was a winner. I must have the recipe. I will even do your next repair job for free if you give it to me."

– Jose Maximilian San Carlos de Cortez

"Thanks for inviting me to my first Seder. Please add me to your guest list for next year. And I would love the matzoh ball recipe." – Ima Khazzer

"I told everyone in the community people should wear their galoshes to avoid STD's even if they are doing it with a sex robot. The days of going where no man has gone before are over." – Dr. Quackenbush

"It's fun to be a sex robot in a senior neighborhood. I have no shortage of admirers and willing gray panthers."

– Delilah

"Speak for yourself Delilah. I'm only for one man."

– Scarlett

"Even though I was demoted, this is a much better job assignment. I still get to wear my gun and don't have to drive too far. It's great fun to watch Rusty bite your arrogant academentians' asses whenever we hold our outdoor court on your campus. And I love the casino."

– Bailiff (aka former Sheriff Mortimer Froussard)

"I give credit where credit is due. Thanks for giving me the opportunity to bag more Einstonians and send them to Briarwood. It's fun to do involuntary commitments especially when I make money in the process since I am a major shareholder." – Judge Solomon

"OK; I have to admit you two Northerners were a breath of fresh air to this community. However, I still think it was Ned who wrote all of the Captain Anonymous letters that challenged the HOA and my business skills."

– Buford Swindler

"I really enjoyed the trip to Amsterdam for the International Love and Sex with Robots Conference. Bella and I liked sharing a room. I also appreciated overseeing

the Kinkhounds. We had a lot of fun comparing notes with fellow perverts." – Ben Chardonnay

"Ben, you snore! A free trip to Amsterdam – who could complain? The conference was fun and educational. I also got a great deal on vibrators." – Bella Blozkop

"Bella and I had so much fun at the conference. A lot of the guys thought we were half our age. It's great having a buff body." – Ava Sinnlich

"Living at Einstein Meadows is a gas. The trip to Amsterdam was a game changing event – if only I could remember what happened. I enjoyed leading the Stoners team." – Professor Growmore

"I was honored to be part of the Stoners Team to represent my fellow academentians from the Meadows. We smoked a lot, we learned a lot, and we made new international friendships." – Zachariah Denker

"Meeting fellow Stoners from across the globe was a trip literally and figuratively. Our home grown beats their shit any day." – Dr. Coconut

"It was great fun bringing my pet monkey Barry to Amsterdam. He was a tremendous hit with the convention goers. Too bad he tore up the hotel rooms and got us kicked out. But it was worth it!"– Leopold Spieber

"The Amsterdam trip was a unique chance to compare notes with people of other cultures with vastly different perspectives. And they sure do know how to party."

– Siegfried Zynismus

"I wish you two would stop telling everyone that it took me three times to pass my licensing exam. Also please stop making fun of my Psy.D. degree. I am glad I went to the Amsterdam conference on Love and Sex with Robots. Somebody needs to keep you degenerates in line!"

– Dr. Jeannette Gedankenlos

"I'm still annoyed that you didn't choose me to join the field trip to Amsterdam. Is it because you are biased toward Native Americans? You shouldn't be; we are, after all, lantsmen from a different tribe." – Dr. Ray Rising-Sun

YIDDISH DICTIONARY

Alter kocker: crotchety, crabby, old man; old fart

Bubbie: a term of endearment for a Jewish grandmother

Bubba meise: a grandmother's story, old wives' tale

Bupkes: something worthless or absurd

Chutzpah: nerve, ultimate arrogance

Dayenu: it would have sufficient

Fercockt: all screwed up

Gelt: cash

Haggadah: the text recited at the Seder on the first two nights of Passover. Includes the story of the Exodus.

Kishkas: intestines

Lantsman: fellow countryman; fellow Jew

Megillah: making something into a big deal

Mesheguna: craziness, senseless

Mezuzah: a parchment inscribed with religious texts and attached to the door of a Jewish household

Mishegoss: ridiculousness, craziness, insanity

Mitzvah: good deed

Nu: so?

Oy gevalt: oh, how terrible

Oy vey: used to express dismay, frustration, or grief

Pesach Sameach: Happy Passover

Pisher: person with little experience

Plotz: collapse or be beside oneself with frustration

Schlepper: someone who wanders aimlessly; freeloader

Schlemiel: incompetent person or fool

Schmear: a portion of cream cheese to spread on a bagel

Seked: shut up

Shalom aleichem: peace be upon you

Shikkered: very drunk

Tafasta meruba lo tafasta: he who grabs too much grabs nothing at all

Tallit and tzitzis: tallit is the sacred white undergarment of Judaism. Tzitzis are the fringes attached to the tallit, which are meant to remind the wearer of God's commandments.

Tsuris: aggravation and woes

Tuchis: backside

Yarmulke: the skullcap worn in public by Orthodox Jewish men

Zitzfleisch: backside, literally skin touching a surface, for example staying in your seat. Bubbie always said 'you need more zitzfleisch' meaning keep your butt in the chair. Thanks to her encouragement, I learned that skill.

Einstein Meadows ¿Qué Pasó Pop Quiz 2.0

** An academic satire without a quiz? Impossible! I still remember the first pop quiz I experienced in fifth grade. The memory still haunts me because that nasty teacher took away my MAD magazine that I was reading after I quickly finished the test. Hey, you know who you are; if you are alive and reading this, I want my magazine back because it's worth more than the price of this novel! Who says I can't hold a grudge?

However, we are fair! No worries, no grades, no pressure; just for giggles. Answers and criteria for potential awards are at the end of the quiz. You can peek if you want! Don't you just love open book tests?

GOOD LUCK!

1. Who keeps saying, "The South will rise again!"?

    a. Ben Chardonnay
    b. Dr. Coconut
    c. Bella Blozkop
    d. Reverend Vernon Verschwender
    e. Filbert der Dorftrottel

2. Which items from the neighborhood's questionnaire for potential new residents would violate the federal Fair Housing Act?

a. What political party do you affiliate with?
b. Where do your ancestors come from?
c. How much do you weigh?
d. What is your net worth?
e. All the above

3. Who refers to the Einstonians as the 'mental masturbators of the universe'?

    a. Members of Congress
    b. Dr. Quackenbush
    c. Ned
    d. Dr. Freud
    e. c. & d

4. Who said "All we see or seem is but a dream within a dream?"

    a. Dr. Freud
    b. Carl Jung
    c. El Sabio
    d. Edgar Allen Poe
    e. Rod Serling

5. What language dictionary is at the end of the novel?

    a. Mexican   b. Greek   c. Yiddish
    d. Chinese   e. Martian

6. What was Judge Solomon's favorite punishment?

    a. 20 push-ups
    b. Three laps around the neighborhood center
    c. Community service for six months
    d. Involuntary commitment at Briarwood Sanatorium

7. When Sister Misty pulled out her vintage "flick my dick" penis-shaped cigarette lighter, how did the assembled group respond?

a. Loud guffaws   b. Shouts of burn it down
c. Running for the exits   d. Plotzing

8. Why did Ned think sex dolls will replace dogs as man's best friends?

a. You don't have to walk them
b. You don't have to feed them
c. They won't tear up the furniture
d. They only require silicone spray
e. All of the above

9. Who was the team leader of the Kinkhounds at the International Congress of Love and Sex with Robots?

a. Filbert der Dorftrottel
b. Ben Chardonnay
c. Dr. Freud
d. Ned
e. Bella Blozkop

10. Why did Filbert want a sex doll for a wife?

a. He was tired of paying $500 for each hour of escort service
b. He wanted a low-maintenance babe with high-maintenance looks
c. He wanted a true soul mate
d. He preferred girls who don't talk, just moan and groan
e. All of the above except (a)

11.What type of equipment was required for dumpster diving?

a. Ladder
b. Surgeon's gloves
c. A grappling iron
d. A Jeep with a winch
e. Protective goggles
f. All except (d)

12. Which of the following titles is not an epiphany in this book?

a. Progress not perfection
b. Everyone must own up to the consequences of their actions
c. People can't dance at two weddings with one behind
d. Be careful what you wish for

13. Who requested a male sex doll?

a. Ima Khazzer   b. Ben Chardonnay
c. Filbert der Dorftrottel   d. Cara Chasid

14. Who volunteered first to lead the group to Amsterdam?

a. Leopold Spieber
b. Buford Swindler
c. Dr. Coconut
d. Ms. Lilith

15. Who called Filbert a genuine pervert?

a. Dr. Freud   b. El Sabio   c. Jeannette
d. Brunnhilde Meeskeit   e. Siegfried Zynismus

16. How did Leopold sneak Barry into the hotel in Amsterdam?

a. Through the back entrance of the hotel
b. In a large suitcase
c. Dressed him up as a baby who Ava wheeled in a carriage
d. Delivered him in a large crate with air holes

17. What did Barry do that got both groups kicked out of the hotel?

a. Got loose and banged on hotel guests' doors
b. Chewed up the sofa
c. Stole the chambermaid's cleaning wagon
d. Took charge of the elevator

18. What did Lillian find in the dumpster that she cleaned up and sold on eBay?

a. Cell phone
b. Purse
c. Vibrator
d. Christmas ornament

19. What was Ima Khazzer's favorite dish at the Engel's Seder?

a. Roast beef
b. Turkey
c. Corned beef
d. Matzoh ball soup

20. Who arrived as Elijah at the Seder?

a. Dr. Quackenbush
b. Jose Maximilian san Carlos de Cortez
c. El Sabio
d. Judge Solomon

21. Which workshops did the Kinkhounds attend?

a. Why not marry a robot?
b. Coolest robots to have sex with today
c. Reflections on moral challenges posed by a childlike sex robot
d. Sex robots and ethical issues
e. All of the above

22. Who said that "when all else fails, Judge Solomon prevails"?

a. Dr. Freud   b. Filbert der Dorftrottel
c. Zachariah Denker   d. El Sabio   e. Sister Misty

23. What is the real moral of the farmer and the donkey fable?

a. Life is going to shovel all kinds of dirt on you
b. Each of our troubles is a stepping stone
c. Free your mind from worries
d. When you try to cover your ass, it always comes back to get you

24. Why does Judge Solomon frequently send people to Briarwood Sanitorium?

a. He believes in mental health
b. His sister is the head psychiatrist
c. He thinks they are all nuts
d. He is a major shareholder
e. c and d

25. Who did sister Misty live with when she escaped from the Sheriff's car?

a. a mountain hermit
b. a traveling salesman in an RV
c. monks
d. guerilla ganja growers

**A Word of Reassurance: Regardless of how you score, you're in good company. After all, we've had politicians rise to high offices claiming they graduated at the top of their law class, when they were actually at the bottom. In this case, only you know how you did. It's ok if you want to say you had a perfect score. Who are we to judge?

Answer Key:	<u>1</u>: d	<u>2</u>: e	<u>3</u>: e	<u>4</u>: d	<u>5</u>: c

<u>6</u>: d	<u>7</u>: d	<u>8</u>: e	<u>9</u>: b	<u>10</u>: e

<u>11</u>: f	<u>12</u>: c	<u>13</u>: d	<u>14</u>: a	<u>15</u>: c

<u>16</u>: c	<u>17</u>: d	<u>18</u>: c	<u>19</u>: d	<u>20</u>: b

<u>21</u>: e	<u>22</u>: d	<u>23</u>: d	<u>24</u>: e	<u>25</u>: d

If you correctly answered:

*   <u>At least 22 questions</u>, award yourself an honorary doctorate. You can choose your specialty. For those of you who already have a doctorate, a second one can't hurt (as Ned will attest). Plus, you've earned a seat on the Einstein Meadows magic bus. Go to the head of the Class!!

*   <u>At least 12 questions</u>, you've earned a seat on the Einstein Meadows magic bus. Great job!

*   <u>At least 10 questions</u>, (tsk, tsk) it's time you reread the book. You are in danger of being listed in Brunnhilde's dreaded Hall of Shame.

*   <u>5 or less questions</u>, Reread the book immediately! You are at high risk of being placed in the community stockade. Remember, in the Southwest, it gets mighty hot. And, don't forget about the scorpions, tarantulas, rattlesnakes, mountain lions and other unfriendly critters.

It's easy to raise your score. We suggest you read the novel aloud with a friend (or two or three). Enjoy your favorite beverage or herbal treat to enhance the experience.

ABOUT THE AUTHORS

Ned and Nancy Engel wrote and published *Einstein Meadows: The Unspoken Perils & Thrills of Living in a Retirement Community*, to which this book is the sequel. They sold hundreds of copies of their debut novel, which is still sold at www.einsteinmeadows.com, www.amazon.com, and www.barnesandnoble.com. Their first novel received many glowing reviews and a strong acknowledgment from a Writers' Digest judge; check out their website to read the reviews. The Engels enjoyed presenting their novel to enthusiastic audiences around the country.

Ned Engel is a licensed board-certified psychologist who has had many articles on creating systemic change published in professional journals. He has always been wonderful storyteller. He believes in the therapeutic power of stories and has presented at conferences in the United States and Canada. He holds two doctorates, a Ph.D. and an Ed.D. The American Board of Professional Psychologists awarded Ned the Diplomate in school psychology. He is a life status member of the American Psychological Association and a fellow in the American Academy of School Psychology.

Ned served as a senior supervisor for both clinical and school psychologists. While he was teaching Master's level school psychologists, he helped his classes create several therapeutic board games for children and adolescents. The Creative Therapy Store sells "Solution City" and "Puzzled." Look for the games at: www.creativetherapystore.com

Nancy Engel has a B.S. in Journalism and worked in publishing for more than 35 years. She was the managing editor of *Popular Photography* magazine and an associate editor of *Fine Gardening* magazine, where she wrote and edited dozens of feature articles. She wrote five chapters of *The Resourceful Gardener's Guide* published by Rodale, and several hundred weekly columns for the *Poughkeepsie Journal*. Nancy also edited 14 gardening books, overseeing the process from recruiting authors through production and bound book. One of the first books she edited won a design award from the Garden Writers Association.

Ned and Nancy enjoy playing electric guitars and billiards together, as well as canoeing, pontoon boating, hiking, biking, swimming, yoga, and target shooting.

**Please visit our website: www.einsteinmeadows.com

**Email us at <u>createmiracles@einsteinmeadows.com</u>

* * * * *

REQUEST FOR REVIEWS

Dear Reader,

We need your help so readers everywhere can share in the joy of Einstein Meadows! You, yes you, have the power to propel the Einstein Meadows movement all the way to Hollywood!

It's so easy. Simply write a review of Einstein Meadows ¿Qué Pasó? on Amazon www.amazon.com and/or Barnes and Noble www.barnesandnoble.com; then crown your review with 5 Gold Stars. Simply search for our book on Amazon.com and Barnes and Noble.com. Click on reviews, then click on write your own review. Neither Amazon nor Barnes and Noble require that you purchase the book from them; anyone can post a review.

We wouldn't ask without offering you, dear reader, something in return. If you let us know you posted a review, we'll send you the soon-to-be coveted magic decoder, which unlocks a deeper level of meaning for the book – the secret of the character of the characters. And, if that's not enough, we'll save you a seat at the premier screening of the Einstein Meadows movie. That will be a real happening. But we need all of you to turn that dream into a reality.

And, if you haven't done so already, please post a review of Einstein Meadows: The Unspoken Perils & Thrills of Living in a Retirement Community while you're there. Amazon and Barnes and Noble sell both of our books.

Peace and love, Ned & Nancy

*　*　*　*　*

ORDER MORE BOOKS NOW

EINSTEIN MEADOWS ¿QUÉ PASÓ?

Lessons Learned While

Letting It All Hang Out

EINSTEIN MEADOWS:

The Unspoken Perils & Thrills of

Living in a Retirement Community

Visit: www.einsteinmeadows.com
Click on the Order Books Tab

** Books in stock
**Autographed Copies
**Volume Discounts

Paperback books are also available on:
www.amazon.com
Kindle eBooks: on Amazon.com

Thank you, dear reader.
Peace and love, Ned and Nancy